By Tessa Dare

LORD DASHWOOD MISSED OUT

By Tessa Dare

Castles Ever After
Romancing the Duke
Say Yes to the Marquess
When a Scot Ties the Knot

Standalone
The Scandalous, Dissolute, No-Good Mr. Wright (novella)

Spindle Cove
A Night to Surrender
Once Upon a Winter's Eve (novella)
A Week to be Wicked
Beauty and the Blacksmith (novella)
A Lady by Midnight
Any Duchess Will Do
Lord Dashwood Missed Out (novella)
Do You Want to Start a Scandal (Coming in 2016)

LORD
DASHWOOD
MISSED OUT

A Spindle Cove Novella

TESSA DARE

AVON IMPULSE
An Imprint of HarperCollinsPublishers

EPub Edition DECEMBER 2015 ISBN: 9780062458285

Print Edition ISBN: 9780062458292

10 9 8 7 6 5 4 3

For Mr. Dare,
who would probably forget the sherry,
but definitely knew a good thing when it hugged him.

ACKNOWLEDGMENTS

I have the amazing Jill Shalvis—and some high-school guy too wrapped up in himself to notice a good thing—to thank for this story. Even though "missed out" isn't strictly Regency usage, Jill's line inspired this story and she was gracious enough to let me borrow it.

Jill, you were so right: Chuck missed out!
Happily, your many fans are much smarter than Chuck.

CHAPTER ONE

By the age of three-and-twenty, Miss Elinora Browning had given up on wedding vows—instead, she made herself a promise. Never again would she place her happiness in the hands of an unfeeling, disinterested man.

Unfortunately, that did not prevent unfeeling, disinterested men from wreaking havoc with her schedule.

"What do you mean, the stagecoach is already gone?"

"Well, miss. It's like this." The coaching inn proprietor scratched behind his ear. His fingernails were cracked and yellowed. "The coach you were meant to travel by, it was here. And it done left. An hour ago."

"But why?"

"The weather looks to be taking a nasty turn. All the other passengers were assembled, so the driver decided to get ahead of the storm. You can take the next one."

"When's the next one?"

"Tuesday."

"Tuesday?" Nora's heart sank. "Sir, I must be in Spindle Cove by tomorrow. I have an engagement."

The man chuckled. "If you're engaged, why would you be headin' for Spinster Cove?"

"It's not a marital sort of engagement. I've a speaking engagement at a subscription library there. I'm an author."

He blinked at her, uncomprehending. As if she'd said, *I'm a hedgehog.*

Nora didn't have time to explain. "Is there no way I can arrange alternate transport tonight?"

"By private post chaise, if you've the coin."

She clutched her purse. Hiring a private coach from Canterbury to Spindle Cove would cost a small fortune. She didn't carry that much money on her person. It wouldn't be safe for a woman traveling alone.

"Please, isn't there anything else traveling in a westerly direction? Even to another location."

He eyed the chalk-dusted slate hanging on the wall. "You may be in luck, miss. There's a gentleman keen to travel to Portsmouth tonight. The coach weren't full yet, but he offered to buy out the empty space. He's leavin' any moment."

"Portsmouth will do, thank you very much. If I can join him so far as Hastings, I can hire a post chaise from there."

The man took her trunk. Nora hurried behind him, dodging puddles as he led the way to a dark, creaking coach hitched to a team of four rather haggard-looking bays. Not precisely a crest-emblazoned, well-sprung barouche.

But when the door swung open, Nora climbed in without thinking twice. Beggars couldn't be choosers.

There was only one other figure in the coach. A man, sitting on the far end of the rear-facing seat, reading a newspaper. Nora positioned herself on the front-facing side, leaving plenty of room for any other passengers who might be joining them.

No sooner had she arranged her skirts, however, than the coach rolled into motion.

As the carriage trundled out onto the highway, she heard the snap of folding newspaper. For the first time, she ventured a glance in her solitary companion's direction. The afternoon's gloom made it impossible for her to make out details.

But Nora didn't need details.

Apparently, she needed a miracle.

She dropped her gaze to her lap and prayed, wide-eyed.

Oh, Lord. Please. Don't let it be him.

But it was. She didn't need to look twice to confirm it.

The other occupant of the coach was none other than George Travers, Lord Dashwood. Nora had suspected it the instant she glimpsed his silhouette.

She'd *known* it from the way her heart raced in response.

She'd always been affected by the sheer size of him. He was hewn from trunks and planks, where other men were carved from branches.

His broad table of shoulders, massive hands . . . They made her feel delicate, the way no one else had ever done. Few would look at sturdily built, fiery-haired Nora Browning and think "delicate." But she was, deep down. There were parts of her spun from floss and held together with hope—and those bits were fragile indeed.

Here was the man who'd destroyed them.

Oh, Lord. Please. Don't let him recognize me.

To be sure, they'd been neighbors in their youths. But he'd been at sea for years, and in the meantime Nora had changed.

Hadn't she? There were fewer freckles on her cheeks. She'd swelled and rounded in the usual feminine places. And despite the years she'd wasted fixating on his capable hands or wavy dark hair, Dash was unlikely to have memorized her features.

He'd never taken much notice of her at all.

"Nora?" His familiar baritone shook her to the core. "Miss Nora Browning, is that you?"

She steeled herself to face him. "Why, Lord Dashwood. What a surprise."

And thus they began a brief, polite exchange that in no way indicated the years she'd spent pining for him, nor the way he'd departed so callously, much less the manner in which he'd once, on a long ago afternoon, reached for her hand beneath a table and twined his fingers with hers.

"I didn't realize you were back in England," she said.

"I've been in Town since late October. I hope your parents are well."

"They are both in good health, thank you."

She couldn't say the same for herself. After all this time, his face was still distressingly handsome. Her stomach wanted to squeeze through the window and escape.

The lengthening silence chastened her. It was Nora's turn to ask a polite question, but she couldn't inquire after his family. Dash had been orphaned as a young boy. He'd inherited his barony while she was still playing with dolls.

Instead she asked, "You're bound for Portsmouth?"

"Yes. Looking in on a new ship under construction. Sir Bertram has charged me with leading the next West Indian survey. And you?"

"I plan to change at Hastings. I'm traveling to Spindle Cove. It's a seaside resort. Popular with a certain set of young ladies."

"Ah."

She turned to the window and peered desperately into the rainy afternoon. There. They'd conversed. Etiquette was satisfied, and now she might travel in peace.

What more was there to say? He'd doubtless left any thoughts of her behind when he left England, and now she was nothing more to him than that Browning girl from down the lane. Andrew's bothersome little sister. The one with the carroty hair and hoydenish ways.

So long as he hadn't . . .

Oh, Lord. Please. Please, don't let him have heard of the pamphlet.

He cleared his throat. "I understand you have turned your talents to writing."

Drat.

"Indeed," she answered slowly. "I wrote a letter to a newspaper a few years ago. The editors liked it so much, they published it as a pamphlet. It has received some notice."

She promptly kicked herself for minimizing her own accomplishments. Hadn't she told many a group of young ladies to do the reverse? *Have the courage to claim your victories,* she always encouraged them.

"I mean to say," she added, "the pamphlet has sold a large number of copies. Several thousand, as a matter of fact. But it circulated mostly among ladies, and you've been traveling for years. I would not expect you to have heard of it."

In fact, I would be most thankful if you had not.

"Oh I've heard of it," he said. "Every woman in London seems to be speaking of it. A number of the men, besides."

He slid down the seat, until he sat almost directly across from her. In the cramped coach, his long legs were nearly bent double. His knee brushed against hers.

And her foolish heart leapt.

Old habits never went away.

It had always been thus, for as long as she could remember. He'd been the lord-next-door, and Dash was a great favorite with the entire Browning family. He and her brother Andrew—God rest him—had been fast friends. Her father had praised the young baron's quick mind. Her mother lavished attention on him as she would as an adopted son.

As for Nora . . .

Nora had simply, stupidly adored him.

How could she not? Dash was clever, strong, and bold. He answered to no one. And God above, was he handsome. Hair black as a raven's wing, curling just at his collar. Equally dark eyes, set beneath heavy brows. A wide, expressive mouth. Add to all this, a voice that had darkened intriguingly as he grew from a boy to a man.

Andrew's death in a riding accident had devastated their family. But Dash had continued visiting Greenwillow Hall, studying Greek and geometry with her father before leaving for university.

When he promised to call on Nora during her season in Town, she had let herself harbor the silly hope that her moment had come. At last, perhaps he would see her—truly *see* her—not as a bothersome, freckled country girl, but as a cultured, sophisticated woman. His equal. And then . . .

And then he'd fall in love with her, of course.

No, No. And then he'd realize he'd *always* loved her, deep down. Just as she'd always loved him. That was the true fantasy. She might as well admit it to herself. Courtship, marriage, children. She'd dreamed a whole life with him.

Well, it hadn't quite gone that way.

Dash's treatment of her that season was so thoroughly abominable, it made Nora nostalgic for the sensation of being ignored.

A few months later, he disappeared from her life completely.

He'd accepted a place with a cartography expedition and left England with scarcely a word of farewell. Nora had felt rejected, worthless.

And—as the months went by—she grew angry. With Dash, with the world, with herself.

One lonely evening, after drinking a touch too much sherry, she sharpened a quill and attempted to purge her feelings on paper. By first light she'd put the finishing flourish on an essay. A literary vindication for every young woman who'd pinned her hopes to a man and then watched both man and hopes walk away.

She squeezed her eyes shut and prayed anew.

Oh, Lord. If you can grant me one plea, let it be this one: Please, please, please. Don't let him have read that pamphlet.

"Your pamphlet made for quite interesting reading." His voice had a frosty edge.

Nora slid her eyes heavenward. *Really. Do you ever answer these things?*

"What was it called?" he mused, tapping his finger on the seat rail. "Oh, yes. *Lord Dashwood Missed Out.*"

"Actually, the title is *Lord* Ashwood *Missed Out*."

"Yes, of course." He fixed her with a stern glare.

She tried to escape it by turning to look out the window, but the small pane was too foggy. She huffed a breath and rubbed the glass with a corner of her sleeve.

All the while, she could sense him staring at her.

"Are you ill, Miss Browning? You've turned quite pale."

"Coach travel rarely agrees with me."

"Pity. Is there something I might offer to increase your comfort?"

"Thank you. I find that silence is the best medicine."

He made an amused noise. "Then I shall let you have your silence. That is, just as soon as you've answered one question to my satisfaction."

The back of her neck tingled.

He leaned forward, bracing his elbows on his knees, confronting her. Caging her. Forbidding her to escape.

And now the tingling made its way down her spine, bringing her every nerve to awareness.

"What, precisely, did I miss out on?"

CHAPTER TWO

"**B**ollocks."

With a baleful look at the gray clouds overhead, Pauline gathered her cloak about her shoulders and hurried across the village green, dodging raindrops as she went.

When she clattered through the door of Brights' All Things shop, she was glad to see a familiar face—and a flash of sunny hair—behind the counter.

Sally Bright looked up from her work, glimpsed Pauline, and then dipped in an exaggerated curtsy. "Good afternoon, Your Grace."

"You know how I hate it when you call me that."

"Of course." Sally gave her a cheeky look. "That's why I do it."

Yes, Pauline understood that. And she couldn't help but smile in response as she unknotted the drawstring of her cloak. She and Sally were the oldest of friends, and old friends teased one another—even when one of them kept a dry goods shop and the other had become a duchess.

"Has the mail coach come through?"

"Not yet." Sally returned to her work, arranging a row of Christmas ribbons on a prominent shelf. "No doubt it's delayed by the weather."

"That's what I feared."

"Why, were you waiting on something in the post?"

"Not a letter. But I'm worried about the roads. Miss Browning is supposed to arrive today. You know, the visiting authoress?"

"Certainly I know her. I like her. She sells. I ordered in a dozen extra copies of her pamphlet. Sold every last one, and I've just received a dozen more."

Without turning, Sally tipped her head toward a stack of slender pamphlets encased in plain brown board.

Pauline walked to the display and picked up the topmost folder. She opened it to see the defiant title: *Lord Ashwood Missed Out: A Gentleman's Rejection, Rejected* by Miss Elinora Browning.

"No surprise that one's popular with the Spindle Cove set," Sally said.

"Indeed."

Spindle Cove had long been a refuge for "unconventional" young women—the bookish, the awkward, the heartsick, the painfully shy. In short, any well-bred young lady who didn't quite fit in with London society.

As a serving girl who'd somehow married a scandalous duke, Pauline counted herself foremost among the odd ducks. From time to time, Griff needed to spend a few weeks in London, but she certainly didn't fit in there. She would far rather be here in Spindle Cove, surrounded by her friends and children—and close to her sister Daniela, with whom she managed the Two Sisters subscription library.

Miss Browning's visit was the first in what Pauline hoped would be a series of literary salons. An attraction during the seaside village's low season. However, if their first authoress failed to appear, the series would not be off to an auspicious start.

And Daniela would take the disappointment to heart.

In a village of unique young women, Pauline's sister was perhaps the most different of all. Despite being a grown woman, Daniela had the understanding of a child. She struggled with speaking and complicated sums, and she was deeply wounded when long-awaited pleasures didn't go as planned.

Pauline let the pamphlet fall closed. "Well, I can't just stand about fretting. Too much to be done. Daniela is still readying the shop. The children are at home with their grandmother. I must go over to the Bull and Blossom to see how the biscuits and cakes are getting on. Griff is due back from Town. He's bringing the sherry."

"Sherry? If you're serving spirits, even I might attend."

"It's Miss Browning's favorite. Supposedly too much sherry one evening is what gave her the courage to write this." She tapped the pamphlet on the counter.

Sally took the pamphlet from Pauline's grasp and leafed through it. "This was more than sherry. Something tells me the woman brash enough to give a wealthy lord a published rebuke isn't about to be cowed by a bit of typical English weather. It's not even three in the afternoon. She'll make it through. It's only a touch of rain."

Pauline peered out the window, wishing she shared her friend's certainty. "It looks as though it's turning to snow."

"**W**ell?" Dash prompted. "I'm waiting."

Keeping his arms braced on his knees, he interlaced his fingers in the center and drummed his thumbs with impatience.

I have you now, Nora. You won't escape.

"I'm sorry, what was the question?"

"You published a pamphlet alleging that I missed out. What, precisely, did I miss out on?"

She didn't answer, which irritated him.

More irritating by far, however, was the way his mind starting filling in answers of its own.

Those lively eyes. That fiery hair. That damnably tempting body.

He recalled her being powerfully tempting, of course, but he'd taken to attributing those memories to his own youthful randiness. To an adolescent boy, even a shapely table leg looked arousing.

And surely she would have aged and changed. *He'd* aged and changed. The tropical climate and sea crossings had weathered him.

But Nora wasn't weathered. She was as pale and rosy and deliciously curvy as all of his memories—only more so. The only noticeable difference he could find was the scarcity of freckles on her cheeks and neck. Had they faded, he wondered? Or had they merely migrated south like a flock of sparrows, seeking warmer climes beneath the tropic of her neckline?

His gaze wandered downward. Perhaps if he were to grasp the tight-fitting cobalt velvet of her traveling frock and rip it seam from seam—laying her bare—he would discover them.

He shook himself. Erotic fantasies were all well and good, but not when they involved Nora Browning.

He didn't want to want her. Not after what she'd done. Not after what she'd *written*.

"The pamphlet?" Her lush, pink mouth broke into a nervous smile. "I hope you can understand, Dash. That wasn't about *you*."

He stared at her with incredulity.

The nerve of her denial. The unmitigated cheek. He was almost impressed by it.

"Not at all," he said, playing along. "I understand completely."

"Oh." She exhaled. "I'm so glad."

"Obviously Dashwood and Ashwood are entirely different names."

"Well, I meant to say—"

"Just because you penned a petty, vindictive screed about a handsome young lord of your acquaintance . . . a lord whose title happens to be a mere consonant different from my own . . . it would be absurd of me to suppose I was the inspiration."

The rain pelting the carriage picked up strength, growing from a mere patter to a proper din. A gust of frigid wind swayed the coach on its springs.

She squared her shoulders and looked at his knee where it pressed against hers.

Was he intimidating her?

Good.

"Lord Dashwood, there's no need to be angry."

He leaned back, stretching his arm along the back of the seat. "Why would I be angry? Just because the name Dashwood—beg pardon, the name *Ashwood*—is now synonymous throughout England with 'vain, self-important jackass who can't observe what's beneath his own nose.' I can't imagine why that would inconvenience me. I mean, it's not as though that reputation might damage my standing in my chosen profession of cartography, in which a man's success rather stands or falls on his powers of observation."

Her head made a pensive tilt. "*Has* your career suffered?"

Dash couldn't believe the way she phrased that question. As if she *cared*.

He examined his fingernails from a distance. "I answer to Travers with my colleagues, and I hadn't any imminent plans for a Dashwood World Atlas. So no."

"Well, then. No harm done."

"To the contrary, Miss Browning. Harm has been done. Not to my career, perhaps. It's my other plans you've muddled."

"Which plans were those?"

"My plans to marry."

"You . . . You plan to marry?"

"Yes, naturally. It's what a man in my position must do. I have a title and an estate. Both require a legitimate heir. That means I need to marry. I'm surprised that I should have to connect these points for you. I always believed you were more clever than that."

Her chin lifted. "And I always believed you to be above cheap insults."

Oh, she had a lot of gall, upbraiding him about insults. She'd published an entire pamphlet that was one long, extended insult to his name. Then sold thousands of copies.

She said, "I'm not sure why anything I do would hamper your efforts to marry."

"Don't you?"

"No."

He decided to humor her. "Now that I've reached the age of five-and-twenty, my uncle no longer holds the estate in trust. It would be irresponsible of me to embark on my next expedition without starting on an heir. However, I have no time or inclination for a long campaign of courtship, and you've convinced the unwed ladies of London—even the aging, undesirable ones who might not otherwise be choosy—that they *deserve* wooing."

Her burst of laughter surprised him. He found it unexpectedly disarming. Something warm and familiar, in the midst of the storm.

"You can hardly expect me to apologize for that," she said.

"Then perhaps you'll apologize for this: If it weren't enough to have encouraged a trend of defiant spinsterhood, you have convinced all the eligible ladies that I, in particular, am a vain, doltish jackass."

"Dash, I am trying to explain. The pamphlet wasn't about you, it was—"

"The devil it wasn't. Enough of this prevarication. You think I don't know, Nora, that you harbored a silly little *tendre* for me all those years? Of course I did. It was obvious."

She went silent. A flush of red suffused her throat.

"You were infatuated. It's a common enough condition, but I thought girls were supposed to grow out of it."

"And I thought boys were supposed to grow out of cruelty. Apparently some still enjoy prodding harmless creatures with sticks." Her eyes flashed in the gloom.

Oh, he recalled those eyes. They worked like flint. Or gunpowder. They were a cool, bluish-gray by default—but when provoked, they shot sparks of green and amber.

He'd hurt her.

Well, and what if he had? Dash refused to feel guilty. He was the aggrieved party here, and he deserved answers.

"Lord Dashwood, please. It's clear you're not interested in listening to any of my explanations."

"You're wrong. I would be interested in your explanations, but I have no use for lies."

She shook her head and looked down at her hands. "It's useless. You will never understand. At Hastings, I will disembark to change coaches, and you will continue to Portsmouth. We will go our separate ways, and we need never speak again. Can we please simply suffer the remainder of this journey in peace?"

"Fine," he replied tersely.

"How much further do you think we have? You are the cartographer."

He peered out the window, but he couldn't see anything beyond the gray wall of rain and fog. "An hour. Perhaps two at the most."

"Surely we can endure that much in silence. An hour, or two at most? That's not so very long. It could be wor—"

The carriage made a jolt, cutting her off mid-sentence and giving her bosom an enticing bounce.

Before either of them could recover their breath, the entire coach skidded sideways, careening off the road before lurching to a sudden stop.

She cried out as the momentum flung her forward.

Acting on instinct, Dash moved to catch her. He slid an arm under her torso, just as her forehead set a course to collide with the door latch.

"Nora!"

CHAPTER THREE

Damn, but this afternoon was a frigid witch.

Griff dismounted his horse, tipped the freezing rain from his hat, and cast a glance toward the tavern, with its promises of beefsteak, ale, and a roaring blaze. Instead, he turned toward a tiny shop with a cheery red door.

More than a meal or a drink or a toasty fire—more than anything, really—he needed to see his wife.

A bell chimed as he entered the small, attractive shopfront. "Pauline?"

No Pauline at first glance, but he did spy a most welcome face—that of his sister-in-law, Daniela.

"Don't move, Duke."

"Good afternoon to you too, Daniela."

"Don't move," she repeated, pointing with the mop she held. "Your boots."

Griff looked down at his muddy Hessians with regret. "Ah, yes. Far be it from me to undo your hard work. I shall remain here. But that means you must come to greet me."

Daniela put aside her mop and crossed to him, curtseying and presenting her hand for his customary kiss. Pauline had tried to explain that Daniela and Griff were brother and sister by marriage now, and this ceremony was no longer required. But Daniela thrived on routine, and Griff rather enjoyed their little ritual. He'd never had a younger sister of his own to spoil.

Pauline emerged from the storeroom, wearing a dusty apron and looking frazzled from her cleaning efforts. Much the way he'd first seen her, on the day they'd met.

He was dazzled, once again.

God, he'd missed her.

For her part, she looked at him with horror. "For God's sake, don't move an inch."

"I've no intention. Daniela has already put me in my place."

"You've brought in the sherry, I hope?"

He frowned. *The sherry?*

"I—I, er . . ."

Stalling for time, he turned to look about the place. It wasn't merely that the floor was freshly mopped. Chairs and benches were arranged in neat, semicircular rows. Every shelf of crimson-bound books had been dusted and tidied.

A sign on the counter announced:

The Two Sisters welcomes Miss Elinora Browning, author
Join us on the eighth of December, at two o'clock
for an afternoon of conversation, teacakes, and. . .

And sherry.

The sherry Griff was supposed to bring from Town. Damn it.

"Daniela," his wife said, her eyes never leaving Griff. "Please go find that lace tablecloth I keep in the back room."

As soon as Daniela was safely out of earshot, Pauline crossed her arms. "Griffin York. You forgot the sherry."

He rubbed his face with one hand, groaning. "I forgot the sherry."

"How could you? I even wrote you a letter to remind you."

"We've Madeira at the house. Or some very fine port. Surely one of those will do."

"No, no. It must be sherry. It's sherry in the pamphlet."

"I can ride over to Hastings," he suggested.

She shook her head. "There isn't time. Not in this weather, this late in the day. We expected you hours ago."

"I know. I was late leaving Town. I—I stopped in to see a friend."

"A friend." Her brow arched. "Does this friend have a name?"

"Naturally."

"But you don't want to share it."

Griff sighed to himself. He couldn't.

He stepped forward and took her by the waist, swaying her side to side. "Come now," he teased. "Don't tell me you've become a jealous wife."

"Am I allowed to be a frustrated one? We've been planning this event for months."

"I know, darling."

"Daniela's worked so hard."

"I know, I know."

"I have eight dozen teacakes on order from Mr. Fosbury. Mrs. Nichols has her finest suite prepared at the Queen's

Ruby, and all the other rooms are filled with visitors eager to hear Miss Browning speak. The tradespeople are expecting a much-needed day of brisk business, right before the holidays. They're all expecting a grand success, and now"—her voice cracked—"the weather is bad, the roads are worse . . ."

"And some unforgivable bastard forgot the sherry."

"I just hate to disappoint everyone."

And Griff hated to disappoint his wife. But he had.

He gathered her into a hug and pressed a kiss to her crown. "I'm sorry."

She sighed, leaning into his embrace. "It doesn't even matter. Miss Browning's coach was supposed to arrive two hours ago. In all likelihood, she won't make it at all."

He pulled back and slid his hands to cup her face, willing those troubled eyes to clear. "I'm certain Miss Browning will arrive on time."

"No one can control the weather. You can't promise that."

"I can," he insisted. "I'm promising you now. Finish your preparations. Miss Browning will arrive on time."

He would get that scribbling spinster here if he had to cart her from Canterbury himself.

And someway, somehow, Griff would procure some god-damned sherry.

All was silent.

Sickeningly, torturously silent.

Nora's shaken mind groped for understanding. The carriage had come to rest. Not quite on its side, but at a steep slant. The two of them had landed in a tangled heap of limbs on the carriage floor.

Dash.

She wanted to speak to him, call out—but panic had seized her tongue. Her voice refused to work.

"Nora?"

Relief flooded her. She felt ashamed of all those stupid prayers she'd sent heavenward earlier that afternoon. This was the only answer that mattered.

He roused and twisted, as if trying to get a glimpse of her face. His fingers brushed a lock of loosened hair from her brow, and an idiotic frisson of pleasure chased through her.

He'd never touched her so tenderly. No man had.

"Nora," he echoed, his voice hoarse. "For God's sake, answer. Tell me you're well."

She managed a nod. Her whole body trembled. No doubt he was anxious to have her weight off him, but no part of her wanted to move. Lord, this was so embarrassing.

"S—sorry," she forced out. "I–I . . ."

"Hush." His strong arms gathered around her, easing her trembling. "All is well. The coach took a skid off the road, that's all. You're unharmed."

"And you? Dash, you're not—"

He shushed her. "I'm unharmed, as well. It's over."

She closed her eyes. His heartbeat pounded against her cheek, strong and steady. His arms held her tight.

All too soon, those powerful arms flexed, lifting her onto the cushioned carriage seat. He kicked the carriage door open and made his way through.

"I'll just look in on the driver," he told her.

She nodded again.

The door fell closed with a bang.

Alone, Nora collapsed onto the seat cushion and curled into a ball. No matter how tightly she held her knees, she couldn't seem to stop shaking. She closed her eyes and tried to recall the feeling of safety.

And her mind ran straight back to his embrace.

How powerful and unyielding his arms had felt. And well she supposed they would be, after four years of sea voyages. Dash would not be the sort of explorer to remain in his cabin, poring over charts. No, he would be hauling on rigging and battening hatches with the crew—honing his arms to nothing but sculpted muscle and cords of sinew, covered by taut, bronzed skin.

She really shouldn't be thinking of him thus. She'd promised herself she wouldn't entertain foolish dreams like this, ever again. But this wasn't quite a dream, was it? It was a memory.

He treated you so poorly, she reminded herself sternly. *He humiliated you before a crowd of onlookers. He left you and never looked back.*

But then he'd held her, right in this coach. She could still hear his heartbeat echoing in her ears.

The door opened.

She startled, jumped on the seat, and tried not to look as though she'd been recently thinking of muscles. Not muscles in general, and most especially not his.

Snowflakes fringed his eyelashes and dusted his dark, curling hair. "I have bad news, and worse news."

"Oh."

"This damnable storm. The temperature dropped so suddenly, the road is a sheet of ice. We ran into a rut. It's a miracle none of the horses were lamed."

Nora sat up. "I can get out. That will lighten the load. I can even help push us back on the road. I'm strong."

He shook his head. "The splinter bar is damaged. The team can't pull on a broken hitch. And even if that could be repaired, the coachman tells me he's just spoken with a rider forced to turn back before Rye. A bridge is out. Cracked under the weight of the ice."

"Oh, no. What does he plan to do?"

"Unhitch the team. Leave the coach here and head back north to the nearest inn. There's just enough daylight left."

"But you can't mean to suggest we'll walk back."

"No. We don't mean to walk, Nora." He looked her in the eye. "We'll ride."

Ride?

Nora closed her eyes. The very suggestion of riding on horseback made her stomach turn.

"Dash, I can't. I just can't. Not tonight. I haven't ridden on horseback since . . . since we lost Andrew."

She remembered it all too clearly. The mare's frightened whinny. The sick crunch of bone.

The breathless terror.

"You won't even try?"

"I don't think I'm able." She cast a desperate look out at the swirling snow. "If this were the Kentish countryside on a warm summer's morn, perhaps. But to ride a strange horse through a snowstorm, in rapidly failing daylight? And after such a scare."

Surely he must understand. He'd been there, too. No matter what malice he believed her to have committed, he had to have sympathy for this.

"I'd rather stay here in the coach," she said.

"Don't be absurd. You don't even have a cloak."

"I have some woolen stockings in my trunk. With the doors shut up tight I'll stay warm enough."

He stared at her for a moment, eyes dark and intense as midnight. Then he muttered a curse and banged the door closed.

For the next several minutes, she remained still, listening to the noises of the coachman unhitching the team. Then all was silent.

Except for the thudding, frantic beat of her heart.

What had she been thinking, letting them leave without her? Was it too late to run after them? If they kept the horses at a walk, perhaps she could manage to keep up on foot. She had to try.

She'd just finished checking her bootlaces when the door banged open.

Again, she startled, pressing a hand to her chest. "Dash. I thought you'd gone."

"You truly believe I'm capable of such villainy? Abandoning you alone in a snowstorm to fend for yourself?"

"Well. You did leave me without a word once before."

He made a gruff noise. "I thought your little pamphlet wasn't about me."

Nora didn't reply.

"Don't worry, you needn't count this as chivalry on my part," he said. "I could say I'm acting out of long-held esteem for your family. But mostly, I'll be damned if I'll leave you here to scribble the sequel: *Lord Ashwood Left Me for Dead.*" He thrust a big, gloved hand in her direction and made an impatient motion. "Come along."

She regarded him, wary. "Where are we going?"

"There's a cottage some distance off the road. Not really a cottage. I believe it's some sort of gamekeeper's shelter."

"A cottage?"

"Perhaps you'd call it a hut."

"A *hut.*"

"It seems to be uninhabited at the moment. Probably barren inside."

"Well, that's lucky," she said, taking his hand. "One wouldn't want for this abandoned hut to be too comfortable. We might be tempted to stay for a holiday."

He grasped her by the wrist and yanked her to him. Their bodies collided as she stumbled into the snow.

Despite the chill, parts of Nora melted. Oh. Those muscles again.

"It's a structure," he said. "One with walls and a roof, and it will keep us alive until the coachman returns in the morning." He looked down and gave her a cold, strange smile. "Assuming we don't kill each other first."

CHAPTER FOUR

Griff was a duke with a mission.

Immediately after leaving the library, he strode across the green to the Bull and Blossom tavern.

"I don't suppose you've a cask of good sherry?" he asked the tavern keeper.

Fosbury answered in the negative, and Griff thanked him anyway.

"Halford," a familiar voice called to him. "Come sit down and have a hand of cards."

Griff crossed to the other side of the room, where three men sat near the hearth, nursing tankards of ale. His old friend Colin Sandhurst, Lord Payne; Colin's cousin Lord General Victor Bramwell, the Earl of Rycliff; and Rycliff's right-hand man—the hulking, taciturn Captain Samuel Thorne.

Each man held a hand of tattered playing cards, and in the middle of the table were a pile of . . .

Griff plucked one of the gray lumps from the table. "You're playing for rocks?"

"Fossils," Colin corrected, snatching the lump from his hand. "Minerva collected hundreds this week. She can spare a few. These round ones? They're ammonites—worth a half-crown. Troglodytes are a shilling."

"I thought they were called trilobites," Rycliff said.

"Listen, Bram, whose lady is the geologist?" Colin retorted. "Do I try to tell you the names of herbs and such?"

Griff interrupted. "I can't sit down to cards tonight. I'm off to see about this Miss Browning who's speaking at the library. The roads are bad, and her coach has likely been delayed." He glanced at the table. "Also, my purse is light on rocks."

"You're going out in *that*?" Colin tilted his head at the rain-glazed window and made a face.

"Well, since Miss Browning is somewhere out in *that* . . ." Griff tilted his head in the same direction. "Yes."

"You shouldn't go alone," Bram said.

"No, you shouldn't," Colin agreed. "Take Thorne."

Thorne glowered at him. But then, Thorne glowered at most everyone.

Colin threw down his cards, pushed back from the table, and stood. "Joking, Thorne. We'll all go along."

"I don't want to ask that of you," Griff said.

"Of course you don't," Colin said, clapping a hand on his shoulder. "You hoped we'd volunteer. And so we have."

Griff scratched the back of his neck. It was true that four men could search faster than two. But Colin Sandhurst had a way of complicating even the simplest errands.

"We'll all go," Colin repeated, shrugging into his coat. "All the ladies are looking forward to the lecture—which means they'll be grateful to whoever saves it. Now and again,

I reckon we could all use an opportunity to endear ourselves to our wives." He looked to Rycliff and Thorne. "When's the last time you did something heroic for your lady?"

Rycliff smirked. "Last night."

Thorne drained his tankard and cracked his neck. "This morning."

"I didn't mean in bed," Colin said. Under his breath, he added, "Braggarts."

Griff shared the sense of irritation. Before this afternoon, he hadn't spoken—or lain—with his wife in three weeks. He was feeling the strain of separation. Intensely. And that was before he'd gone and cocked up her event by forgetting the sherry.

Much as he hated to admit it, Colin was right. He needed a hero's errand. It had been years now since he'd given up a fortune to be with Pauline, and it seemed like a gesture he should be repeating weekly. But he only had the one fortune to give.

Tonight, he was going to rescue a waterlogged spinster.

"Let's make ready, then," Griff said. "We'll need to be quick."

"I suppose that's true," Rycliff replied, standing. "Otherwise the ladies will solve the problem on their own, as always. Are you with us, Thorne?"

In answer, Thorne rose to his feet.

"Then it's settled," Griff said. "Gather at my house in thirty minutes. I need to look in on my children first."

"Make it an hour." Colin reached for his hat. "I've a few things to do. Saddle my horse. Find my greatcoat. And give my wife two screaming orgasms." He leveled a finger at

Thorne. "I tell you, Mr. This Morning, I won't be outdone by the likes of you."

Nora gathered her valise. "My trunk?"

"Is staying put unless you carry it," Dash answered.

"But—"

He'd already turned away and started walking across a snow-dusted field, covering the ground in long strides.

Nora hastened to follow. She had no choice. What with the swirling snow, she had no idea where they were headed or what she'd do if she found herself alone.

Together, they trudged through the mud and snow. She stumbled into a furrow that was hidden by a thin crust of ice and the dusting of new snow. Ice-cold, muddy water came up to her knees.

By the time they reached the cottage, her damp petticoats had stiffened, and her toes were nearly frozen through.

When Dash pressed against the door and found it barred, Nora's heart became a lump of ice. But he found a small, knotted string to lift the latch and pushed the door open.

He made an ironic bow. "Ladies first."

"H-how long do you think it will take the driver to return?" she asked, ducking through the doorway.

"He won't return until morning."

"Morning?"

She looked about the tiny hut they currently occupied. It was such a small space—no bigger than a closet, really. Just a woodburning stove, a lone stool, and simple table. There was one small, high window—a rough opening with no glass, currently shuttered.

And a single, narrow bed.

She had nowhere to hide. Not from his wrath, and not from her own feelings, either.

"Dash, we can't stay here all night alone. Together."

"If you don't care to stay," he said, "here's the door."

When she made no move to leave, he closed the door and dropped the bar in the latch.

Nora tested the narrow bed with her hand. It creaked, but at least she didn't feel the straw-stuffed mattress shifting with vermin. She lifted a rolled quilt from the foot of the bed and unfurled it with a snap of her arms—just as he turned to face her.

A cloud of dust bloomed, instantly coating his eyebrows and hair with gray powder.

He stared at her, choking on dust. Or possibly choking on his rage.

Nora bit her lip. "Sorry."

"If," he said tightly, standing still as a statue, "you think I'm happy about this turn of events . . . I assure you, I am not."

"I can see that."

Nora struggled not to laugh. With those dust-frosted brows and his stern expression, he looked like a grumpy old hermit. She pulled a handkerchief from her pocket and held it out as a peace offering.

He took it and angrily swabbed at his face. "I would much rather this weren't our situation. Once, while we were sailing around the Cape of Good Hope with Sir Bertram's expedition, a squall came up. We had to lash ourselves to the masts and cling for dear life as massive waves swamped our ship. It was the most wretched, harrowing night I've ever experienced."

"Are you saying you'd rather be there than here?"

"No. I'm saying I'd rather *you* were there than here."

"Really. There's no need to be cruel."

He made an amused sound. "Perhaps there isn't a need. But there's a powerful desire." He swept a look down her form. "You need to undress."

"What? I will not."

He ignored her protest. His hands went to the row of buttons down the front of her traveling frock, yanking them loose, one by one. "Those boots and skirts are soaked through. I'd imagine your stockings are, as well. I can imagine it now. *Lord Ashwood Gave Me the Ague*."

"I'll do it myself, thank you." She put her hands over his, stopping his progress. His fingertips were freezing. By instinct, she rubbed her palms up and down his chilled skin. "Oh, Dash. These hands are ice. You need to warm yourself, too."

Their eyes met and held for a tense moment.

Nora silently cursed herself. Here was the root of all her problems. No matter how poorly he treated her, no matter how little he returned her feelings—her silly heart insisted on caring for him, just the same.

He released her. "I'll make a fire."

She turned away, trying to remove her wet frock, petticoats, and stockings with as much modesty as possible. Dash was right, her legs were soaked to the skin. It was only when her feet started to warm that she realized how cold they'd been. Her toes felt pricked by a thousand needles.

When she was down to her stays and her relatively dry chemise, she wrapped the dusty quilt about her shoulders and sat down on the bed, tucking her feet under her thighs.

Dash had removed his own coat, waistcoat, and cravat, hanging them on a peg near the door. As she watched, he banged about the cabin in male, violent ways. Slinging splits of wood about, jabbing the ashes in the stove with a poker, slamming the woodbox open and shut. So physical. Strong. His broad shoulders strained the damp, nearly translucent fabric of his shirt.

Nora cleared her throat. "Could you—?"

"Could I what, Nora? Cease making a fire? Let you freeze here alone? Don't tempt me."

She set her chin. "Could you let me know how I might be of help? What are you searching for?"

"Tinder." He turned a look about the tiny cabin, and his eyes landed on her valise. "I don't suppose you travel with copies of that wretched pamphlet?"

Nora ignored his baiting words. She removed a flat wooden box from her valise and set it on the table. "I do have blank paper. I'll shred some while you pile the wood."

She opened the travel desk and looked over the contents: Paper, quills, ink, penknife. Taking a piece of paper, she folded it back and forth, again and again, until it resembled a paper fan. Then she took her knife and began to slice it into shavings.

Having piled the wood in the stove, Dash took the results of her little crafting project and strategically heaped it beneath the wood. He struck the flint, sending a spark into the stove. The paper caught easily, and the cheery flame gave Nora hope—but then it dwindled and died. The wood hadn't caught.

"More," Dash said.

Nora took out another sheet and repeated her process. Dash struck the flint and managed a spark. But the flames soon died, just as before.

"Again," he demanded.

This time, as he blew steadily into the tiny paper-fueled blaze, Nora bit her lip. If they didn't get a fire before nightfall . . .

It would be a long, dark night—but not a lonely one. They would be forced to huddle together for warmth.

Nora would rather be lashed to the mast off the Cape of Good Hope.

She rose from the bed and went to his side, crouching next to him, adding her lungs to the effort. They took turns feeding the blaze with their breath, until her sides ached and her head was dizzy.

At last, the wood caught.

Relief washed through her, and warmth and light began to suffuse their small quarters.

Unfortunately, now that the fire was lit, it became clear that a long night stretched before them both. They had no food, no amusements, and little to occupy themselves.

Heaven knew they didn't wish to *talk* to one another.

Dash pulled a silver flask from his pocket and uncapped it before offering it to her. "Brandy."

"No, thank you."

"It wasn't a question." He pushed the flask into her hand. "You need to warm from the inside, too."

Nora accepted a cautious sip. The liquid fire spread through her empty belly, warming her insides and muddling her wits.

She passed the flask back to him, and he tipped it to his lips for a long, greedy swallow. Then another.

Wonderful, she thought. Because drunkenness was exactly what this miserable evening lacked.

He drummed his fingers on the table. A brisk progression of first finger to last. *Tap-tap-tap-tap. Tap-tap-tap-tap.* Over and over.

Over . . .

And over . . .

And over.

Nora set her teeth.

"Do you know any songs?" he asked.

She was silent.

"I know songs," he said, in a lascivious tone. "Sailor shanties, mostly. They're all unspeakably vulgar."

He continued the steady drumming of his fingers. *Tap-tap-tap-tap.*

This was going to be the longest night of her life.

For once in her life, Nora wished she were one of those ladies who traveled with needlework to occupy her hands. Instead, she settled for taking her quills from her writing desk, one by one, and whittling the nibs to arrow-sharp points. Her knife scratched against the quill again and again—a brittle, repetitive sound that was likely to annoy him.

She *hoped* it annoyed him. Two could play at his game.

Scratch.

Tap-tap-tap-tap.

Scrrratch.

Tap-tap-tap-tap.

Scrrrrrrrrra—

Dash whipped a sheet of paper from her traveling desk and reached for the pen in her hand. "Do you know, I believe I shall write a pamphlet of my own. It will be titled *Lord Ashwood Has No Regrets*."

"How clever of you."

"Don't worry." He cut her a sharp look. "I'll change your name. By one letter. To Miss Frowning, I think."

"You would not help your cause. I am a figure of public sympathy. You would only cement your image as a villain."

"Better a villain than a laughingstock." He dipped the pen and continued to write. "But this is hardly the extent of my revenge. If you think my pamphlet is bad, just wait until I sue you."

"*Sue* me? For what?"

"For libel, naturally."

"You can't sue me for libel. The truth is a defense against libel."

"There was nothing of truth in that screed. The entire thesis of your pamphlet is faulty."

"How so?"

He set the pen aside. "I took the opportunity to expand my knowledge, use my talents, and explore the world—and yet you say I missed out? Because I didn't stay within five miles of my birthplace and settle down with the girl next door?"

He held out his hands, palms up, like a pair of scales with his options weighed on either side.

He lifted one hand. "A world of adventure." He lifted the other. "You."

Nora stared at him. How dare he?

She'd laid herself bare in that pamphlet. It had terrified her merely committing the words to paper in the solitude of her room. Allowing it to be published was her greatest act of courage in life, and so much good had come from it. She'd come away with friendships, respect, a career of sorts—as much as gentlewomen were permitted to have careers. Women from all over England and beyond wrote to her, expressing their gratitude.

"I will not allow you to treat me this way," she said. "You're not the only one who explored his talents these recent years. I have attained a certain measure of success."

"Yes. You did." He leaned forward. "And you used me to get it. Shamelessly trampled my good name for your own petty reasons. I would have every justification for exacting revenge. In writing and in court. Unless . . ."

"Unless what?"

"Unless you can prove it."

"Prove it?"

"Demonstrate to my satisfaction that I missed out on something. Anything." He crossed his arms on the table. "We're here, and we do have all night."

What?

If he was suggesting what he seemed to be suggesting, he was a rogue. "You can't mean to force me to—"

"I'm not forcing anything. But answer me this. If I missed out on something so wonderful, how do you explain the fact that every other man in England is equally dense? You could have married elsewhere by now. Surely some man would have seen what I did not."

She pulled the quilt about her shoulders. "I have been too busy for dances and courting."

"Too busy creating a reputation as a manhating virago, you mean. I suppose that *would* scare lesser men away."

Lesser men?

What was that phrase meant to signify? He probably hoped she would ask. Nora decided to refuse him the satisfaction.

To be truthful, the last few years *had* been too busy. She simply hadn't any opportunity for courtship. Even if she had, no gentleman had caught her eye. She thought perhaps she'd grown out of infatuations and would never be interested in any man.

But here Dash was again, being maddeningly interesting.

Not merely interesting.

Captivating.

Now that the firelight had filled the small hut, she had the opportunity to study him. She was fascinated by the map the world had drawn on his body, while he was out mapping the world. Small, squinting lines around his eyes, and a thin scar on his forearm, and tanned skin that gave way to a slightly paler hue above his wrists, and on the exposed wedge of his chest.

He tapped the table in impatience. "I'm waiting. What is it I missed?"

She cleared her throat. "To begin, you missed out on a partner who is your intellectual equal. In London, you surrounded yourself with those brainless beauties."

"Surely you, champion of the female sex, don't mean to argue that beautiful women cannot also be intelligent."

"No. Of course, I should never say *that*."

"Good. Because if you attempted to make such an absurd

statement, I could produce a dozen examples of beautiful *and* intelligent women to disprove it."

"That won't be necessary."

Ugh. The last thing Nora wanted was to hear a recounting of his many beautiful, clever lovers. The very thought made her stomach churn.

"In fact," he said, "I needn't look beyond this cottage. I could begin the list with you."

CHAPTER FIVE

Dash watched closely as her cheeks darkened to a satisfying blush.

"What?" she said.

"You," he repeated. "You are a woman who is both intelligent and beautiful."

She was obviously flustered by this statement.

He was right. She didn't know.

It made him perversely happy that she didn't. He liked being the one to tell her. It meant no other man had.

"You never noticed me. Not that way."

Wrong again, Nora.

He had noticed her, even then. When she'd tagged along on his fishing excursions with Andrew. During all those mathematics and Latin lessons she'd wheedled her way into joining. She was always in the periphery of his view.

Now she'd come into focus. Eyes bright and keen, skin cleared of all its youthful spots. Womanly curves in full abundance.

"I mean, I do believe you gave me some credit, intellectually. When we were younger, you had great respect for my mind."

He choked on a laugh. To be sure, he'd known she was clever. But her mind wasn't what had distracted him from his geometric proofs, much less what had haunted him during restless nights. "Whatever gave you that idea?"

"There were so many times when my father would ask you to come to the slate, and you would sit back and say, 'I don't have the answer, but I suspect Miss Browning does. Let's allow her to have a go.' Don't you recall?"

"I recall."

"Why else would you do that?"

"Because I couldn't go to the slate. Not without embarrassing myself."

"Don't be absurd. I know you must have known the answers. You were always so quick with figures."

He rubbed his eyes. "Oh, Nora. I was sixteen years old. My figures weren't the reason I declined to go to the slate. It was your figure."

"I don't follow you."

"I was a randy youth. You were a blossoming young woman. Do you understand me now?"

She stared at him blankly.

Apparently he would have to spell this out.

"You"—he extended both hands in her direction, vaguely cupped—"had breasts. I"—he slapped his palms to his chest—"had erections."

She blinked. "What?"

Oh, for the love of God. "When a man is aroused, his—"

Thankfully, she cut him off with a gesture. "I understand how the anatomy works. I just can't believe I did that to you."

Always.

She'd always done that to him. Hell, she was doing it to him now. Between the brandy, their state of undress, and the enticing shadows the firelight cast below her ear and between her breasts . . .

Desire gripped him. Hard.

He was losing his patience for coy banter.

"Suffice it to say," he said, "beauty and intelligence are not so hard to come by in one person. And it's been many years since I noted both qualities in you. So again, I ask—how can you justify this scurrilous pamphlet? What did I miss out on?"

She looked as though she would speak. And Dash knew what she wanted to say.

At least, he knew what *he* wanted her to say.

Come along, you evasive minx. Out with it.

In the face of her silence, he had no choice but to call her bluff. He picked up the quill and dipped it. "A lawsuit it is."

My heart, Nora wanted to shout. *You missed out on my heart.*

Just watching him scratching away at the paper, she was transported back to their youth. She'd passed many hours peering around her brother's bowed head to watch Dash scrawling on his slate. He wrote so awkwardly, with his left hand all curled up. Unlike most children, he hadn't been forced to use his right. At seven years old, he was already an orphaned baron. Who could force him to do anything?

Dash's left-handedness had dictated their seating arrangement. He sat to the left of Andrew. Nora sat to the right. Otherwise, they all bumped elbows.

How many times had she had sat at that table, daydreaming about Dash's strong hands or dark eyelashes, and wishing there was no Andrew between them?

Then came that dreadful day when there wasn't any Andrew between them, and she'd rued her every wish.

Nora wasn't the superstitious sort. She knew her brother's death wasn't her fault. It wasn't anybody's fault, not even the horse's.

Accidents happened.

But after he died, the lessons stopped. It seemed the end of everything for Nora, too. She'd not only lost her brother, but Dash's company—and now she would lose the chance to further her learning. Her father had humored her desire to join while he instructed the boys, but he would see no reason to educate Nora on her own.

She would never forget the day when Andrew was a fortnight in the ground, Dash came to call. She hurried down the stairs to find him standing in the entrance hall, his lesson books tucked under one arm.

He'd bowed and addressed her father. *Sir, shall we continue as before?*

They'd proceeded to her father's study, taken seats in their usual chairs. Dash on the left. Nora on the right, and that horrible, empty space between them. And somehow they'd struggled to continue. Not only with lessons in mathematics and Greek, but with life.

While her father chalked an example on the wall-mounted

slate, Dash reached beneath the table, bridging that empty gap, and took Nora's hand.

Oh, she'd been infatuated with him for years.

In that moment, infatuation had become love.

They worked that way for hours. Fingers twined beneath the table in secret whilst they continued writing with their favored hands. And for every minute that ticked away on the clock, Nora's heart was another mile gone.

There was no undoing it. She saw that now.

Her heart was his, and it always would be.

But she was terrified to tell him so. What if he'd known her heart already, too—just as he'd known her mind and her body—and yet he'd still chosen to walk away?

"Dash," she whispered. "You missed . . ."

He threw down the quill. "What did I miss, Nora. What?"

Faced with his impatient, glowering expression, she lost her nerve. The stakes were too high. If he rejected her again, she didn't know how she'd bear it.

But there he was, waiting on her answer.

Something wild and stupid took hold of her. Pride, she supposed.

"Only the greatest pleasure of your life." She let the quilt fall from her shoulders, tossed her hair, and thrust out her chest. "We would have been magnificent lovers."

Chapter Six

For the third time, Pauline rearranged sweets on the plate before her. Spice biscuits, seedcake, small iced petit fours.

She sat back to look at them and consider the symmetry of her display. Then she picked one up and stuffed it in her mouth.

"Oh, don't!" Charlotte Highwood cried. "There'll be none for tomorrow."

"There are four more trays in the kitchen," Pauline muttered through a mouthful of cake. "But the event will likely be canceled anyway."

"Don't worry," Kate said. "All four of our men out there searching for her. They can't fail."

Charlotte popped a biscuit into her mouth. "Remember, one of those four men is Colin."

"Colin can be surprisingly resourceful at times," her sister Minerva replied, wife of the troublemaking viscount in question.

"It just feels strange that we're all sitting here eating cakes," said Susanna Bramwell, Lady Rycliff, helping herself to the sweets. "Feminine empowerment is the reason I began inviting ladies to Spindle Cove. It's the reason you've invited Miss Browning to speak. And here we are, waiting for the men to save the day."

"Men do want to feel needed from time to time," Kate said.

"Speaking of men feeling needed"—Minerva paused in the act of bringing a seedcake to her lips—"did any of your husbands seem oddly . . . um . . . determined before they left this evening?"

"Now that you mention it," Susanna replied slowly, "Bram did seem rather focused on a goal."

She, Minerva, and Kate exchanged knowing glances.

"What?" Charlotte asked. "What is it?"

Declining to answer, the three married ladies each bit into a teacake.

Pauline couldn't help but feel envious of their blushes. Griff had been gone for what felt like ages, and they hadn't had any sort of proper reunion. She felt guilty for the way they'd parted. Right now, they could have been rolling in bed, and instead he was somewhere out in the cold.

Mrs. Highwood roused herself from a nearby table and joined them, knocking a third teacake out of Charlotte's hand with her fan. "Do stop stuffing your face, Charlotte."

"But Pauline is worried. We're consoling her—and ourselves." Charlotte frowned at her mother. "And why do you have a fan, anyhow? It's snowing outside."

"My nerves know no season." Mrs. Highwood fanned with vigor. "I, for one, am happy if Miss Browning never arrives. It's shocking. Teaching young ladies that they needn't marry to have value? Rejecting the opinions of gentlemen? Appalling. If she did arrive, Charlotte, you would not be permitted to attend."

Pauline watched Minerva and Charlotte exchange an exasperated glance. The Highwood sisters were no stranger to their mother's nerves, nor her loud opinions on marriage. One would think having her eldest two daughters happily wed would allow the matron to relax about Charlotte's prospects.

On the contrary, Mrs. Highwood seemed to have redoubled her determination.

"Don't look to this group for advice, Charlotte," the older woman said. "Or if you must look to them, heed their example, not their words. They know the importance of an advantageous match." With her folded fan, she gestured to Susanna, Minerva, and Pauline in turns. "Married to an earl, viscount, and duke."

"But we married for love, Mrs. Highwood, not advantage," Susanna said.

Kate raised her hand. "And I chose a soldier when I might have married a marquess."

"More to the point, your own eldest daughter married a blacksmith!" Charlotte cried.

"Diana married an artisan," her mother corrected. "And don't remind me." She flicked open her fan and worked it furiously. "So help me, Charlotte. If you run away with a butcher before you even have your first season . . ."

"I've no intention of running away with a butcher. Nor a baker, nor a candlestick maker. Unlike my sisters, I enjoy dancing, and I'm fond of parties. I'm heartily looking forward to my season."

"Thank heaven. I knew I'd given birth to one daughter with sense."

"In fact," Charlotte continued, "I hope to have at least five seasons in Town before I even think of settling down."

With a dramatic moan, Mrs. Highwood sank into a chair and reached for a cake.

"**M**agnificent," Dash drawled. "We would have been magnificent lovers. This is your argument."

"Yes."

"You, an untried, gently bred virgin, know how to please a man. Better than any merry widow or courtesan."

A shiver went through her. Nora started to worry about whether he meant to call her bluff—and how she meant to respond, if he did.

Nevertheless, she couldn't back down.

"I don't care how many lovers you've taken, nor how experienced they were." She held up her index finger. "I have more passion in one fingertip than they have in their whole bodies."

He propped an elbow on the table. A smile played at the corners of his lips. "Why, Elinora Jane Browning. What on earth have you been doing with that fingertip?"

"Wouldn't you like to know." She kept her tone saucy, trying not to betray her nerves.

"I think I would, yes."

His gaze made a slow journey up her body, lingering on the swell of her breasts where they overflowed her corset. Her pulse raced, and her breathing quickened.

How did he do that? He didn't even need to touch her. He

didn't even have to speak. Just a sweep of those intent eyes, and her nipples drew to tight points, chafing against the linen of her shift.

He noticed.

"It's cold in here," she said, inanely.

"Well," he replied. "We can't have that."

Dash rose from the table and walked around it, coming to stand before her. The entire journey took three paces, but for Nora it was an eternity. Tension built between them. Her nipples were aching now, and a dull pulse throbbed at the juncture of her thighs.

Slowly, deliberately, he retrieved the quilt from where she'd tossed it aside, shook it out, and then draped it around her.

"There." He tucked the blanket about her shoulders. "Better?"

She didn't know how to answer. Her senses were muddled by the scents of brandy and leather and musk. She couldn't stop staring at the gaping open collar of his shirt, and the intriguing whorls of dark hair it framed.

"Nora." His voice was husky. Intimate. "If you think the idea of seducing you never crossed my mind, I assure you— you're wrong. Quite wrong."

"Then what stopped you?"

He took a step backward, breaking her trance. "My good breeding, of course."

"Your good breeding. Please. What part of your good breeding was on display when we were in London?"

His mouth pulled to the side. "Yes, London. That was badly done of me, I'll admit."

"Badly done," Nora parroted, mimicking his deep voice. "You promised my father you would look after me in Town. I waited three weeks at my aunt's in Berkeley Square before you even deigned to call. And when you did, you appeared in her parlor unshaven and reeking of brandy. Worse, French perfume. But I forgave you everything because you were there, at last, and you invited me to a night at the theater with your friends."

He rubbed a hand over his face.

"Finally, I thought. Here is the London season I dreamed about. You must know I never much cared for balls or dancing. I longed for culture. Experience. The opera, exhibitions, salons. I wanted to be a part of an exciting new circle of society, and you were my only way in. I spent four hours readying myself for that night. My best silk. New gloves. Every lock of hair in place." She laughed at herself, remembering. "I so was worried about embarrassing you. I addressed my reflection in the mirror in German, French, Italian. I read the week's newspapers, twice. And then . . ."

"And then I took you to the theater. Just as I'd promised."

"Oh, yes. You did. We shared a box with your wastrel Oxford friends and their lightskirts. They rudely laughed and chattered through the entire first and second acts. You ignored me. I watched a woman in scarlet wedge a wine flute in her décolletage. And then I watched you drink from it."

"I was a jackass that night. I know it."

"I know you know it. You did it all on purpose, in public, in a calculated fashion, clearly with the aim of disappointing me. Wounding me. What I want to know is why."

"You don't already know why? You, who claim to know me better than I know myself?"

"I want to hear you say it."

Dash was silent.

Her quiet fury only built. "My father made excuses for you, you know. When I returned home still weeping and humiliated, he tried to tell me you were hard-hit by Andrew's death. You poor young man, how you must be grieving."

"He was correct. I *was* grieving."

"My mother consoled me, too. All men your age needed to sow a few wild oats, she said."

"And your mother was right, as well. I was a man of two-and-twenty, wealthy, with normal appetites and few checks on my behavior."

"You were a coward," she bit out.

He flinched.

"You were a coward. You knew I had hopes. Hopes that were shared by my family. Rather than let me down gently, privately—as basic respect might have demanded—you decided to make me a spectacle instead. To humiliate me publicly. To make me a fool."

"I was callow, I readily admit. Immature. So were you. You had unrealistic, girlish expectations. I know how the female imagination works, leaping from attraction to matrimony in a heartbeat. In your mind, you were probably naming our children and choosing new carpets for Westfield Chase. Embroidering 'Lady Dashwood' on your trousseau."

"You're wrong," she hedged. *About some of it.* "I detest embroidery."

Also, she'd only chosen girl baby names. She'd been planning to let him name the boys.

"I did have respect for your family," he said. "And for you.

A great deal more respect, I daresay, than you have shown me."

"You had respect for *me*? Oh, that is rich. That display in London aside, when you accepted the position with Sir Bertram, you never even bid me farewell."

"I paid a call at Greenwillow."

"And you spoke to my father, yes. I heard you downstairs."

"You were out, I assumed."

"You knew I was there. I came hurrying down to greet you. I told myself I should have more pride, but I couldn't help it. And yet I was too late. You were already out the door. I stood there in the entryway, watching you all the way down the lane. You never once looked back."

Her eyes burned. She forced herself to take a deep, slow breath. Long ago, she'd vowed to herself—she would not shed another tear for him, ever again.

"I used to daydream," she said. "About what would have happened if I'd rushed after you that day, caught up to you in the lane . . . I could have made you stay. I could have changed your mind."

"Nora." He exhaled her name as a weary sigh. "You could not have made me stay."

"You can't know that."

He was silent for a long moment. "Very well, then. Have your chance now."

"What?"

"Whatever it was you would have said or done. Let's hear it now. You said you played the scene again and again in your mind."

"Well, if we're going to play the scene," she said, "you must do your part. You were leaving."

"Fine." He walked to the door and lifted the wooden latch. "Here I am, leaving Greenwillow Hall."

He opened the door. A blast of cold invaded the small cottage, bracing and fierce.

"This is your chance, Nora. Convince me. Give me a reason I should stay."

With one last, daring look at her—he left.

She went to the open door, watching him walk away from her for the second time in her life. Making big footprints in the drifting, swirling snow.

Not looking back.

"Far enough?" he asked, not turning.

"Further," she called to him. "Keep going."

His figure grew smaller and fainter as he stomped into the snowy night.

For a moment, Nora contemplated slamming the door and barring it. She didn't need to prove herself to him. Not anymore.

She stood there, watching. He never slowed. Never once looked over his shoulder. As though he would desert all over again. Growing smaller and smaller, melting into the dark night.

Let him go, she told herself.

But something in her heart twinged and snapped. Like a strand of India rubber pulled to its limits, then released. It stung. It pulled her off balance. And before she knew what she was doing—

"Wait."

She gathered the hem of her chemise, lifting it to her ankles, and charged out into the snow, calling his name over the howling wind.

"Dash! Dash, wait."

By the time, she caught up to him, she was breathless. She

put her hands on his shoulders—those broad, strong shoulders—to turn him toward her.

"Wait. Don't go. Come back inside." She slid her arms around his neck. "Stay with me."

And then she kissed him.

As many times as she'd thought of this moment . . . dreamed, schemed, choreographed, imagined how she would persuade him to stay . . . none of it mattered. Her actions were entirely instinctual, driven by impulses and needs deep inside her.

They came from the heart.

She pressed her lips to his, and a touch of frost between them quickly melted to fire. Delicious, intoxicating, brandy-flavored warmth. She wanted more. It didn't even concern her that he was standing as still as if he were frozen, not responding. She'd wanted to touch him for so long, and now her hands were on the strong column of his bared neck, her fingers twining in his dark, unruly hair. She tasted his lips, tilting her head to the side and stretching to make herself taller. Pressing light kisses to his mouth, again and again.

"Stay," she whispered between kisses. "Stay with me."

The freezing wind caught the hem of her chemise and tugged it, snarling the tissue-thin fabric about her ankles. She shivered and pressed the full length of her body into his enticing masculine warmth. He was warmer than any fire. As though he'd soaked up the sun of tropical shores and taken it into him, saved it for just this moment—so that he might give it back to her on this cold, snowy English night.

She pulled back from the kiss and stared up at him. The faint light from the hut illuminated half his face. He was half light, half darkness. She wanted him for all of it. Always had.

He breathed her name once again.

And this time, it didn't sound like an exasperated sigh or a weary complaint, but like a raw confession. A curse. A prayer.

His strong arms came around her, lifting her up on her toes. And his mouth crushed against hers.

There was no snow. No cold. No wind. No darkness. Only a blazing, white-hot conflagration of desire that seem to light up the whole night.

When at last he lifted his head, she felt certain the earth must be scorched beneath them.

A snowflake landed on her cheek. He touched it with the tip of his thumb.

"Well?" she breathed.

"Sweet, darling Nora." He caressed her face. "I still would have left."

The rogue.

She gave a cry of outrage and kicked him in the shin. Given the thickness of his boots, the gesture did more damage to her toe than to his shin, sadly. But it helped immeasurably with her pride.

She tried to wrest out of his embrace, but he held her tight.

"Listen," he pleaded. "You should thank me."

"I'll thank you to release me and then leave, as you've declared you'd prefer to do."

"What would our lives be like, if I'd stayed? Asked for your hand, as I knew you hoped. As I knew would please your parents. As I was tempted to do myself."

He was tempted? Tempted to marry her?

He read her mind. "Of course I was tempted, Nora. Yours was the only family I'd ever known. You can't imagine how much I longed to make that a permanent connection. But that wouldn't have been fair to you. You would not want to be married for your family, nor for security."

She rolled her eyes. "So now you've done me a favor. I'm to be *grateful*."

"Yes. Would we have been content? I suppose so. Perhaps even happy. But we would never have pushed our boundaries, become our best and bravest selves. I would not be a cartographer. You would not be a writer."

He put his hands on her shoulders and pushed her back from him, letting his gaze flicker down her form. "God, look at you. You're famous. Wanted for speaking engagements all over Britain. It's remarkable. You're remarkable. You don't need me for entrée into salons or exhibitions. You don't need my admiration, either."

"But I can't stop wanting it." She stamped her bare foot against the snow. Cold prickled through her toes. "That's what makes me angriest of all. Don't you see? I'm still that eighteen-year-old girl inside, wanting to be noticed. No matter how rudely you treated me once, or how many years have passed, or how much I've accomplished, I can't stop craving your good opinion. I can't stop myself from missing you, worrying over you when you're gone. Wondering what you would think about an article in the paper, or whether you'd laugh at a joke. It's not a matter of logic, or I would have solved it long ago. The problem is in my heart. I'm still . . ."

"Still what?" he prompted.

"Dash." She swallowed hard and met his eyes. "Do you really not know? I've always been in l—"

Slam.

CHAPTER SEVEN

They were plunged into total darkness.

Dash was disoriented completely. That kiss—and she'd been wrong; "magnificent" didn't begin to describe it—had muddled his wits. He felt as though he'd been swept up in an Atlantic squall, tossed around a few hundred times in the hold of a ship, and then dumped in the Sussex countryside.

Within a few moments, reason returned and the cause of the darkness dawned on him. Behind them, the cottage door had slammed shut.

Nora gasped. "Oh, no."

"Don't worry," Dash assured her. "The framing's not level. But it's only swung on its hinges. That's not a problem unless the—"

Bang.

The noise shuddered down his spine.

"Unless," he said, "the bar drops in the latch. Like that."

Blast.

Blast and damn.

Dash forced himself to be calm. Perhaps it wasn't so bad as he feared.

Releasing Nora, he strode to the door and gave the wooden panel a push.

His push met with resistance. Firm, solid, unyielding resistance.

Blast and damn and hell. Wretched luck. The bar had fallen squarely in place, and earlier that evening he'd drawn in the string meant to lift it. In doing so, he'd thought to keep them safe.

Hah.

Nora rushed to his side. She rattled the door, finding no more success than Dash had made moments earlier.

She turned and looked up at him, wide-eyed in the dark. Ice crystals clung to her lashes. Her dilated pupils seem to reflect the sense of dark, fathomless doom welling in his gut.

She was an intelligent woman, and she knew as well as he that their situation was dire.

They were locked out of their only shelter. In the cold. Dressed in little more than their skins.

And there would be no one coming to their aid. Not until morning, at least, and by that time, they'd be frozen through.

Blast and damn and hell—those words were insufficient now.

Dash had spent much of the past four years on a ship. He could blaspheme in a dozen different languages, and in that moment he mentally rattled through curses in each and every one.

But for Nora's sake, he refrained from speaking them any of them aloud.

"Fuck," she said.

The word hung in the air, sharp and clear as an icicle.

Dash laughed, and suddenly the despair felt a little less. "A lady shouldn't know that word."

"A lady shouldn't *use* that word," she corrected. "And I'll admit, I never have used it before. But what have I been saving it for, if not this moment?"

Fair enough.

He nodded in grim agreement. "Fuck."

She gave him a smile full of chattering teeth and wrapped her arms around her torso. "At least the next time you find yourself lashed to a mast during a gale off the coast of the Cape of Good Hope, you'll be able to say, 'It c-could be worse.'" Her dry laugh made a worrisome cloud.

He longed to clutch her to him, skin to skin. Warm her with his body as best he could. But that wouldn't last long.

The best he could do, rationally, was to find a way inside. Get her near a proper fire.

"Stand aside," he said.

"What for?"

He didn't bother to answer. He needed to conserve his energy for action, not talk.

He fell back one, two, three paces. Then he dug in his heel, gritted his teeth—and made a fierce charge toward the door, using his lowered shoulder as a battering ram. When he collided with the wooden panel, pain reverberated across his shoulders and down his arm.

The door rattled, but the latch didn't give.

He backed up and tried again.

When he collided with the door a second time, Nora gave a choked cry of something that sounded like distress.

"Dash, don't. You'll be injured, and that won't help anything."

"If I don't get us inside," he said, retreating for another attempt, "we'll both be dead."

He rammed the door a third time, this time aiming for the hinges. Perhaps they would be more persuadable than the latch. Again, the oaken slab rattled but refused to yield. And again, the pain exploded like buckshot through his arm and down his back.

He growled with frustration.

"George, please."

George.

She only called him that when she was afraid.

"As entertaining as this is to watch," Nora suggested, "perhaps we should look for another way in. There was a window."

He shook his head, even as he walked around to the side. "It's so small. More of a vent."

"I think I could squeeze through, if you were to boost me."

"It's latched, too," he said, raising both hands to the shutter and rattling it. "From the inside."

Dash kicked at a drift of snow. It didn't help, but it felt good.

He needed to make a plan.

"We'll go back to the coach. At least it's some shelter from the snow and wind, and your trunk is there. Perhaps there's a rug or two for warmth."

"It's too far," she said. "And it's dark now. The snow has covered our path. We could stumble around for hours."

"Not for hours. We'd freeze long before that." He passed a hand over his face. "Jesus Christ."

He slid her a look. His eyes had adjusted to the darkness, and there was just enough glimmer of firelight leaking through the cabin's cracks that he could make her out.

She was so pale. Perhaps it was merely a trick of the dark and the moonlight—he hoped to God that was the case—but her lips looked a deathly shade of blue.

And good Lord, she was still barefoot.

He pulled her to him, roughly, enfolding her in his arms and setting her feet atop his boots. He moved his arms briskly up and down, trying to soothe her shivering.

"I'm so sorry," she said, burying her face in his chest. "This is all my fault."

Now *that* was an uncharacteristic statement. He was really and truly concerned about her. She was going demented in this cold.

"You're wrong," he told her. "The fault is mine."

All mine.

In more ways than she could possibly know.

"No, no. This was my notion. My silly game. Go out and kiss in the snow? With scarcely any clothes on? What a stupid idea." She lifted her head. "Why didn't you tell me it was a stupid idea?"

Ah, so now it was a little bit his fault after all. Despite the cold, he felt the corners of his lips pull into a smile. This was the Nora he recognized.

"I suppose," he said, "because I rather fancied the idea of kissing you in the snow. With scarcely any clothes on."

"We've always had a connection. Haven't we?"

He nodded.

"We could have been good together. Tell me you felt that, too."

He nodded. "Yes."

"I knew it couldn't have been just my imagination. At least I'll go to my grave knowing I was right on that score."

A violent shudder went through her, and then the shivering ceased. That couldn't be good.

The tips of his ears had gone numb, and frost stung at his nose and lips. He pulled her head tight to his chest and buried his face in her hair.

"Be calm," he whispered.

"I can't be calm. We have to do something." She perked with a sudden surge of energy. "I'm not going to go easily."

No, my darling. You never would.

"We were always best at solving problems as a team." She turned to investigate the window and its frame. "Of course the hinges would be inside. We can't remove it altogether."

"And it's too high for me to try battering it in. If I had an axe, I could break through." He pushed at the seam of the two wooden panels, testing the latch. "If we could manage a slender lever of some sort, perhaps we could ease it through the gap and lift the hook."

She tugged at his sleeve. "My c-corset. There's a whalebone busk down the center, just here."

She drew a line from the midpoint of her sternum to her navel, tracing the shape of a narrow bar.

He framed her rib cage in his hands, running a thumb down the inch-wide spur of whalebone. "That just might do the trick. We only have to get it out."

He curled his fingers under the two cups of her corset and pulled them in opposite directions.

"You mean to rip it in half?"

"I'll have it in a moment." He braced his feet, took a stronger grip, and tried again. "This stitching . . . is remarkably . . . strong." He let go and stood back, breathing hard. "How *do* pirates manage their plundering?"

She giggled. "I don't know about pirates, but I know seamstresses sew these with a little p-pocket." She guided his fingers to the valley between her breasts. "Just here. To slide the busk in and out."

His fingers took hold of the pale, thin divider, and out it slid. "Ah. I see. That does make more sense."

"I would have thought you'd know your way around a lady's undergarments."

Dash shook his head. There wasn't time to discuss this now. Nor was there time to contemplate the exquisite softness of her breasts.

"I'll boost you." Lunging one boot forward, he made his knee into a stepstool. "Like so. You'll have to wedge the shutters apart with your shoulder and sneak the busk through."

"I know." Her teeth chattered.

"Are your hands warm? Because if you bobble that thing and drop it inside before the shutter's unlatched, we're finished."

"I *know*. But I'm not getting any warmer."

Dash wasn't convinced. He took the busk from her shaking grip and caught it in his teeth. Then he yanked up the hem of his shirt and pulled her chilled hands flat against his abdomen before drawing their two bodies close.

God above. It was a good thing he had something to bite down on. The shock of her icy hands against his torso was torture.

But soon, they began to warm. To soften. She rubbed up and down, tracing the ridges of his tensed abdominal muscles with her fingertips.

Those wicked fingertips, each filled with a woman's worth of passion.

This was torture of a different kind.

"I'm ready," she said. "I think that's enough."

No, no. That wasn't nearly enough. He wanted those hands on him everywhere.

But first, he wanted to get inside.

"Just keep steady," she said, bracing one hand on his shoulder in preparation. "If I'm halfway through this little operation and you falter, the shutter will smash my fingers right off."

"And you'd never hold a quill again. That would be a shame."

She gave him a horrified look.

"I'm only joking. Nora. *Nora.*" He reached for her in the dark. "I swear to you. I'll never hurt you again."

He touched her cheek, and was appalled by its icy pallor.

"Let's continue this conversation inside. On three, now. One, two—"

She stepped on his knee, and he pushed her plump little backside up onto his shoulder. Then he did his best impression of a stone gargoyle whilst she wiggled the sliver of whalebone through the shutters' gap.

"Any progress?" he grated out. The muscles in his shoulders were knotting.

"Almost have it," she said, her voice dreamy. "It's moving."

Dash gritted his teeth against the pain and dug his heels into the snow. "Take your time."

With a creak, the shutter gave way, spilling a square of yellow light onto the snow.

"Brilliant," he said, gathering one arm around her knees and putting his hand under her backside. "Now I'll boost you up and through."

She glanced down at him. "Promise you won't look up my shift."

"It's freezing. We're in danger of dying of hypothermia. Stealing a glance up your shift is the last thing on my mind."

She made a sound that communicated doubt.

Well-founded doubt, Dash had to admit. Even though it was true that the two of them were in danger of freezing to death, stealing a glance up her shift was not the *last* thing on his mind.

It wasn't even near the last.

It might even be among the top three or four things on his mind, were they ranked.

After all, it sounded like a nice way to die. A little glimpse of heaven before the lights dimmed.

Nevertheless, he marshaled what remained of his gentlemanly reserve to rebuff the temptation.

One more growl and flex from him, and she was halfway through.

"Slowly now," he warned as she eased her knee over the window's edge. But the wind and cold stole his words. He didn't hear her respond.

In fact, he didn't hear anything . . .

Until a dull, heart-stopping thud.

To wait out the snow, then. Right.

CHAPTER EIGHT

Griff pulled his gelding to a halt at a crossroads. Colin, Bram, and Thorne did the same, clustering around him for direction.

It had to be well past midnight, or so Griff assumed. He wasn't sufficiently curious to unfreeze his fingers from their clutch around the reins and go fishing his pockets for a timepiece.

It didn't matter how late it was. It was dark and cold, and the horses were trudging more and more slowly through the snow. And despite a thorough survey of the past twenty miles, they yet hadn't found any sign of the stagecoach or Miss Browning.

"The coach would be coming from that way." He nodded in the direction of the east fork. "We'll continue to follow the route in reverse, stopping in at each turnpike, inn, and tavern to inquire after them. Either their progress is slow, or they stopped somewhere to wait out the rain."

"Snow," Thorne corrected, brushing a fresh dust of flakes from his sleeve.

"To wait out the snow, then. Right."

Griff jammed the brim of his hat down over his eyes, trying to shield himself from worry. Neither rain nor snow was foreign to Sussex roads. The drivers and teams managed to keep their schedules in inclement weather all the time. If everyone in England stayed home for a spot of rain or snow, no one would ever go anywhere.

"Let's be on our way, then."

"Wait," Colin said. "I think we need a name."

"A name?"

"A name. You know, for our group. We might as well be a cricket team or a crime gang, so long as we're wearing these." He indicated the poorly knitted, violet-and-green-striped muffler about his neck.

The mufflers were a gift of Griff's mother, the Dowager Duchess of Halford. The woman was a menace to yarn.

"We don't need a name," Bram said.

"No, we don't *need* one," Colin said. "But it would make this little outing immeasurably more entertaining."

Griff nudged his horse into motion.

Colin was, as ever, undeterred. "How about the Sons of Debauchery?" he suggested, his voice carrying over the wind. "Or the Lost Lords. The Fallen Fellows? The Hellraisers. Oh, I know. The Duke and His Dissolutes."

Griff shook his head. The Duke and His Dissolutes? That last was a bit too close to describing his old life. Before Pauline, he'd surrounded himself with the worst sorts of reprobates. Colin Sandhurst among them.

Was it any wonder she'd doubted him when he'd refused to name his mysterious friend?

"We don't need a name," he repeated.

"A musical theme, at least?"

"No."

This answer came from Griff, Bram, and Thorne in unison.

Colin harrumphed. "I'm telling you, you lot have no sense of adventure."

They stopped and dismounted to let the horses drink. The layer of ice glazing this creek was the thickest they'd encountered yet.

"Don't worry," Bram said. "If she stopped this far east, that means they stopped before the worst of the weather hit. She's likely snug in an inn somewhere near Rye."

"Probably," Griff agreed.

And he knew forcing his friends to continue this quest was folly.

"You should turn back," he told the three of them. "Take shelter in that pub we passed a few miles ago. Warm yourselves before heading home. I'll go on alone."

Thorne cursed.

"What my friend means is, this is nothing," said Bram. "We're infantrymen. We marched over the Pyrenees in the dead of winter. Twice." He slid a glance in Colin's direction. "Can't speak for my cousin, though."

"I'll have you know, I traveled the full length of Britain in under a fortnight," Colin said, clearly not wanting to be outdone. "Some of it by public transport. There was mud."

Joking aside, Griff knew that Colin didn't like traveling by night—and for good reason. But he was here out of friendship, and so were Bram and Thorne.

The size of his social circle might have declined in the years since he'd married a serving girl, but the quality of friendship had grown immeasurably.

Thorne said, "Lead on, Your Grace."

As Griff moved to mount his horse, he noticed a light winking at them from the far side of a distant hill.

Fresh tracks of horses and wagons—several of them—led in that direction.

"What's that?" he wondered aloud. "Some kind of inn?"

It would seem unlikely that Miss Browning would take shelter so far from the main road, but there were few stopping places along this stretch of highway. If the weather had taken a sudden turn, they might not have had a choice.

"Might as well have a look," Bram said.

As they approached, it became obvious that the building was some sort of stop for travelers—or had become one, due to the storm. Lights burned in every window, and the hoof-prints of several horses led toward the barn. Sounds of conversation and the clink of dishware came from within.

Maybe this was it. Perhaps they'd found her.

And perhaps there would be dinner in it, too.

They tied their horses to a post in front, then stamped the worst of the snow and mud from their boots as they headed for the front entrance.

As they approached the door, Colin sidled up to him. "How about this? The South Sussex Scoundrels."

Griff stifled a groan.

Yes, he was grateful for friends. To a point.

He pushed open the door, leading the way inside. "For the last time, we don't need a—"

The words died in his throat.

They'd entered a large, open room—packed with men grouped in small clusters around tables.

To a one of them, every man in the place went silent, turned, and stared at Griff.

And then they reached for their guns and knives.

A closer look told him the reason. These tables weren't laid with dinner plates. They were heaped with sacks of spices, bolts of silk, casks of spirits.

His eye fell on a small barrel labeled . . . Jerez de la Frontera.

Sherry.

These were clearly smuggled goods—or perhaps a ship had wrecked in the storm, and this was the haul from shore.

Damn. This was no wayside inn. They'd stumbled into a den of thieves.

And all the aristocratic blood in the world wasn't going to rescue them. Even the bluest blood spilled red from a sliced throat.

"What's all this?" A big, ugly mountain of a man rose to his feet. Clearly the leader. His nose and cheeks were pitted with old pockmarks, but his eyes seemed to work well enough. PoxFace surveyed their group from their muddied, expensive boots to their mufflers.

Their stupid, matching striped mufflers.

Colin cleared his throat and addressed the men. "Say, is this not the Ceylonese Mission Society meeting? I'm afraid we've taken a wrong turn, brothers. So sorry to trouble you. We'll just be on our w—"

PoxFace motioned to one of his subordinates.

The door slammed shut behind them. Griff heard the scrape of an iron bar pushing through the latch. A bow and a hasty apology in retreat wouldn't get them out of this.

They'd have to fight their way out. And find a way to take that sherry with them.

Bram cleared his throat, drawing Griff's gaze. His hand went to the pistol at his side, and then his eyes darted in Thorne's direction, indicating that the officer was ready, too.

Colin's hand tightened on Griff's shoulder. "I've a knife in my boot," he murmured. "Bram's saber is yours for the taking."

Griff gave him a tight nod.

"Now," PoxFace sneered. "Who the devil are you lot?"

With a swift, satisfying clang of steel, Griff drew the saber and leveled its gleaming point at the smuggler's pitted nose.

"We're the Lords of Perdition."

Dazed from her fall, Nora attempted to get her bearings. Her cheek was pressed to the floorboards. Her limbs were sprawled at odd angles. Her hair was a righteous disaster.

Lord. She was so, *so* grateful Dash couldn't see her right now.

"Nora?" The door rattled.

Dash.

Good Lord. While she was here preening, he was still outside.

"Nora!" He rattled the door again. "Nora, are you hurt?"

She tried to respond, but her breath had been knocked from her. As she scrambled to her feet, she heard a muffled oath. Then a crash as he rammed the door with his shoulder.

Apparently, he was back to Plan A.

"Nora, be calm. I'm coming for you."

She pushed herself to her feet and hurried to unlatch the door. She managed this just in time to intercept Dash's next attempt to ram the door.

Which meant he ended up ramming *her*.

His eyes went wide, and he tried to stop himself, but the momentum was established. He caught her in his arms, and together they crashed to the floor. They landed in a tangle of limbs and linen. His weight atop hers.

And Nora began to think she would never breathe again.

He searched her face with grave concern. "When you didn't answer or open the door? I thought you'd been injured in your fall."

She shook her head.

"Were you injured just now?"

Again, she shook her head no.

"You're distressingly quiet." His hands moved up and down her body, assessing. "We need to get you warm."

Nora wasn't going to object to that.

Dash lifted her onto the small bed, spreading his coat for her to lie upon and heaping the quilt atop her. Delicious warmth seeped into her chilled body—but even better was his intent, competent focus. The firm confidence with which he moved.

She loved how tender he was being. How he fussed over her, in his brusque, unfussy way.

She was reminded of that afternoon he'd taken her hand beneath the schoolroom table. Dash could be stern and haughty at times, no question. But when it counted, his was a caring soul. And that heart . . .

The woman who won that heart would be rich indeed.

As he tucked the quilt around her middle, Nora winced.

He frowned. "What is it?"

"I landed on my hip when I came through the window. It's probably a bit bruised."

Without hesitation—and certainly without asking permission—he pulled the blanket aside and hiked her shift to examine her.

He turned onto her side, exposing the pale slope of her thigh to the firelight, and ran his fingers over the surface of her skin. Her flesh rippled with tiny bumps. Beneath the quilt, she was aflame.

"Nothing broken, I think."

She shook her head.

"You'll mend?" he asked.

"It would take more than that to keep me down."

His eyes caught hers. "Good."

She laughed nervously. Absurdly. Then, even worse, she wet her lips. Out of desperation, she dropped her gaze and stared at his hand on her exposed thigh. Perhaps when he withdrew his hand, she would regain her sense.

But he showed no indication of removing it. In fact, his thumb slid idly back and forth. Cherishing. Thoughtful.

"Now then," he said. "Let's go back to the subject we were discussing out in the snow. Right after that magnificent kiss, and before the slamming door interrupted us."

Nora couldn't begin to recall. There was nothing in her mind but this moment. His touch. His voice. His warmth.

"You'll have to remind me," she whispered. "What subject was that?"

"You were about to tell me you loved me."

CHAPTER NINE

Beneath the quilt, Nora's heart flipped in her chest. "I was not."

"You were. I know you were."

Her jaw moved, but she couldn't make words.

His gaze pleaded with her, both vulnerable and defiant. "Just say it. Doesn't matter if you stopped long ago. Just say the words this once, and I won't ask again. It's only . . . I can't recall ever hearing them before."

Oh, curse him and his shameless appeals to her romantic heart. One sweep of those dark, needing eyes and everything in her melted to liquid.

"Dash, you must know how we all loved you. You were part of the family."

"And you? Did you love me as a brother?"

Her heart pinched. What would the words cost her now, but pride? And they could mean so much to him.

"No," she said. "I did not love you as a brother. I loved you with imprudent, reckless abandon. I loved you with all the heart and soul I knew how to command."

He dropped a kiss to her bruised hip. His hand stroked down the length of her bared leg, and he curled his fingers around her ankle.

"And then you left," she went on, "and I felt so stupid for it. It made me question everything I believed about myself. That's why I wrote the pamphlet."

"You needn't—"

"No, I need you to know this. I owe you this much. When I said it wasn't about you, I wasn't being dishonest. If you'd allowed me to finish, I would have explained. It was about *me*. I was so heartbroken, and so angry with myself for my inability to forget you. I needed to believe that there was something special inside me. Some reason worth continuing on, when it felt as though everything was lost. First Andrew, then you. All my hopes and plans. I was desperate to pull myself together, find a new purpose."

"You did. You did that all, and more. I'm fiercely proud of you."

"And I'm proud of what you've accomplished, too." She touched his hair. "Envious of it, to be honest. But proud, as well."

"I'm glad to hear it. Your opinion means a great deal to me."

"Does it?" She rested her fingers on his cheek.

"More than you know."

And then his lips touched hers.

He dipped his head to kiss her neck, then her chest. He nuzzled back and forth, easing her chemise aside to expose more of her bosom. The linen slipped from her shoulder, freeing the pale globe of her breast, capped by her dark, taut nipple.

He stared down at her for a long, nerve-shredding moment, his brow furrowed and eyes intent. "So lovely."

Then he bent his head and captured her nipple in his mouth.

Pleasure ripped through her, bright as lightning and leaving her equally shocked. He licked and teased her, drawing circles around the aching tip before taking her in his mouth again and suckling her hard.

Nora's back arched as she was racked by the exquisite sensations.

Meanwhile, he skimmed his hand upward, beginning at the calf and slowly climbing to her knee, her thigh, and then higher. His exploration was slow and thorough. Devastating.

He lifted his head from her breast, his fingers paused on her upper thigh—just at the border between Mere Impropriety and Utter Ruin.

His breath stirred her hair. "Tell me to stop if you don't want this."

She wanted this. She'd always wanted this.

And she made a promise to herself, then and there: No shame. No regrets. No thoughts of the future, either. There would be only wanting and pleasure tonight. Whatever happened between them, the fault or credit would be hers, just as much as it was his.

She shifted on the bed, letting her leg fall to the side, giving him freer access.

Offering him everything.

He slid his hand higher, settling his palm over her mound and parting her folds with callused fingers.

Her breathing grew hot, heavy. He stroked up and down,

inflaming her with desire and spreading the thin sheen of moisture with his fingertips. A hollow feeling built deep inside. She was aching for him.

She pushed through the folds of linen and quilt to find the hard ridge of his arousal. He twisted his hips to help her as she undid the buttons of his falls, freeing him.

As she skimmed one fingertip over the tip, a low moan escaped his throat.

They turned onto their sides, facing one another. Truthfully, it was the only way they would both fit on the bed. Unless one of them were atop the other, of course, and Nora wasn't quite ready for that part.

She never would have dreamed that she could do this without dying of mortification—staring unabashedly into a man's eyes while he fondled her most intimate places and she stroked his. But it wasn't nearly as awkward as Nora had worried it might be. This was Dash, after all. They were merely two people who'd been acquainted all their lives, getting to know one another in this new, thrilling way. She searched every inch of him she could touch, marveling.

A wicked smile curved his mouth. "Well? How do you find me?"

"Large."

He chuckled.

"It wasn't meant as a compliment." She peered down between them, studying the formidable, thick curve of his erection, arcing up toward his navel. "I knew a man's organ hardened, but I didn't realize it swelled so. Are all men like this?"

"Some are smaller. And some are larger, I'm sure."

"You're so hard." She slid her hand slowly down the full length of him, from tip to base. "But soft to the touch."

He leaned forward, kissing her cheek and ear.

"You're soft, as well," he whispered. His thick finger slid inside her, and she gasped. He pushed in and out, a bit deeper each time. "Sleek. And tight. And wet."

He was wet, too. Just a little bit, at the tip. She touched her finger to the bead of moisture and spread it in widening circles. He groaned.

With a muttered oath, he flipped her onto her back, pushing her chemise to her waist and then drawing the garment over her head and casting it aside. He shucked his trousers as well, shaking them off one leg to land on the floor.

"My shirt," he directed, bending to kiss her. As their tongues tangled, she grasped the linen by the hem and pushed upward, helping him disentangle one arm, then the other. He broke the kiss just long enough to pull the garment over his head, then bent to kiss her again.

"Wait," she said, pressing her hands flat to his chest. "Let me touch you."

"If you insist."

He stayed like that, straddling her waist as she skimmed her hands over the sculpted planes of his chest and shoulders. Running her palms down his strong, sinewy arms.

"You must tell me what you like," she said.

"I like"—when she brushed her thumbs over his nipples, he sucked in his breath—"that. I like you. I like everything."

"No, I mean . . ." She gathered the courage to meet his eyes. "I'm not experienced, of course. But I want this to be good. Perfect."

"Nora." He moved his weight forward, balancing on his elbows. "Let's address this right now. It's not going to be perfect."

"But—"

"It's not. We can't be other than we are. You, being you, are already setting unrealistic expectations. You'll likely act on bad assumptions. And I, being myself, am liable to be rash and overbearing." He nestled his hips between her legs, pushing her thighs wide. His lips touched her forehead. "I may hurt you, when the last thing I want is to cause you pain."

"I know."

"So it's not going to be perfect. That doesn't mean it can't be good."

She bit her lip. "I think I promised magnificent."

His laugh was husky and warm. He lowered his body to cover hers.

His strong, hairy leg twined with her smooth, slender one. She kissed his neck, and his shoulders tensed. His hardness pulsed at the cleft of her legs. She could sense how heroically he was struggling to hold back.

Nora reclined against the satin lining of his cloak.

No more conversation.

It must be now.

He reached between them, positioning the broad head of his arousal where they both wanted—no, *needed*—it to be.

Then his hips flexed, and he pushed inside her, just a bit. An inch, perhaps.

Again. Another inch.

Again, and again.

Each time, she gasped for breath. Her fingernails dug into his arms.

He was killing her by increments, filling her and stretching her and hurting her and giving her all of himself. Everything she'd been missing for so long. It was bliss and torture all at once.

At last, he was completely within her, and his heartbeat pounded next to hers.

A sense of rightness settled all the rioting sensations of pleasure and pain. No, it wasn't perfect.

It was exactly what she'd always wanted it to be.

Dash, you idiot. You've made a grave mistake.

Just staring down at Nora's breathless, flushed face, he could have kicked himself. The sensation of her body surrounding his, hugging him in the tightest, most intimate embrace . . . The pleasure was enough to drive him mad. He was thrusting into her, mindless with bliss and years of pent-up need, pushing himself ever closer to the brink.

And he was hurting her, badly.

Which perhaps was unavoidable from the first, but he should have made certain she found pleasure first. Now there would be no chance of her reaching climax.

Unless . . .

Unless she hadn't been lying about the passion in her fingertips.

"Touch yourself," he said.

"What?"

"Touch yourself. Where it pleases you."

He tried to make this voice a deep, dark command. So that she wouldn't even think to question—just assume his to be the voice of experience.

Tentatively, she slid her right hand from his shoulder and worked it between them, settling her fingertips right where their bodies joined.

"Yes?" she breathed.

"Yes." He plunged deeper. "God, yes."

He levered up on his arms and sat back on his haunches, try to give her more room. Well, and also to give himself more space to watch.

What a picture she made. Her fiery hair, her smooth skin. Her long, elegant fingers working between her legs, and her full breasts rolling to the rhythm he set.

Damn. He'd never seen anything so arousing in his life.

It was almost too much. He had to close his eyes for a few strokes.

Think about ice, he told himself. Wind and sleet. Squalls off the Cape of Good Hope. Anything to cool the surging crisis in his loins.

"Dash."

His eyes flew open. She stared up at him, eyes glazed and cheeks flushed. Lips slightly parted.

"That's it," he told her. "Don't stop, darling." He fought the urge to thrust faster. "Don't you stop until you—?"

She cried out and convulsed around him, her inner muscles squeezing his cock like a silk-gloved fist.

And thank God for it, too. He couldn't hold back any longer. Ice and squalls be damned. He leaned forward, tilting her hips to a deeper angle. He knew she'd be hurting tomorrow, but he couldn't resist.

She wrapped her legs around his hips and held onto his neck, and Dash lost all control. He thrust hard and fast, and faster still, until he reached that blissful, dizzying plateau of inevitability.

"Yes," she urged, locking her legs tight around him.

Yes.

And *yes* and *yes* and *yes* again.

He slumped atop her, utterly spent in every way. His limbs were trembling with effort and damp with sweat.

She held him tight, pressing kisses to his shoulder and neck.

Why had he ever chafed against her hopes for them? In this moment, he never wanted to let go.

Nora, Nora.

"Well, what's the verdict?" she said, once they'd both caught their breath. "Am I acquitted of libel?"

He rolled aside and exhaled. "Unequivocally."

"Really?" She propped her chin on his chest and looked up at him. Sparks of amber flashed in her eyes. "You admit that you missed out on something in me?"

He reached out and tangled a hand in her fiery, tousled hair. "I can declare, without a doubt: Best lovemaking ever."

She grinned with satisfaction. "Magnificence accomplished."

"Of course," he said, staring at a lock of her hair as he wound it around his finger, "it was also my *first* lovemaking ever."

"*What?*"

"Do you know, I think the storm has stopped. I don't hear the wind any longer."

"George Travers." She playfully pounded him on the chest. "What are you telling me?

"That what we just shared was, indeed, magnificent. And no matter what happened, it was going to be my best time ever. How could it not be?"

"I don't believe it."

He shrugged.

"You're a lord. A young one, in your prime of life. Wealthy, educated, advantaged in every way. Not to mention, devastatingly handsome. Why on earth . . . ?"

Dash started to feel a bit self-conscious. "It's not as though I didn't have chances, you know. And I'm a hardly a saint. I did a fair amount of groping and ogling of girls at school, went to the typical bawdy shows with the Oxford set."

"You drank champagne from scarlet women's bosoms."

"Yes, that too." And there'd been some minor indiscretions he wouldn't detail. "But when it came to the act itself, I never met a woman I wanted so badly that consummation seemed worth the risk."

"The risk? I thought women bore all the risk. Men who have conquests are heroes. We're the ones who are considered ruined."

"I'm not going to argue it's equal risk, but men take chances, too. Fathering a bastard child. Angering a jealous lover. Contracting some hideous strain of the pox."

"The pox?" She made a face.

He tweaked her ear. "I'm an only child *and* an orphan. I don't have indulgent parents to rescue me from scrapes, nor a brother to fill my place. I had to take care."

"Oh, Dash. As alone as you've been, I can only imagine." She stroked his chest, thoughtful. "Do you want to know what I think?"

"Always."

It was the truth, too. Much as she had a way of maddening him, he would always wish to know what was on her mind.

"I think you feared more than just the pox. Like being vulnerable with the wrong person. Exposing your heart to someone you couldn't trust."

Damn. There she went, maddening him. How did she know him better than he knew himself? It wasn't fair.

"Perhaps that was part of it, too." He gathered her in his arms and buried his face in her sweet-smelling hair, breathing deep. "It's good to be here with you."

She hugged him close. "What are old friends for?"

"Are we friends again, then?"

"Were we friends before?"

"I think so. Friends who spent a great deal of time dreaming about kissing and fondling one another. Which sounds to me like the best sort of friends, come to think of it."

She laughed.

"Now tell the truth." He propped a finger under her chin, tilting her gray-blue eyes to his. "How many were there, and what were their names?"

"How many what? Whose names?"

"Our children. The ones you had all planned out."

"You rogue."

She squirmed in good-natured outrage, and he tickled her into submission, rolling her onto her back.

"I have you pinned," he said, gripping her wrists and holding them over her head. "Just admit it."

She rolled her eyes. "Fine. Five."

"Five?"

"Three boys and two girls."

"And . . . ?" he prompted. "What were their names?"

"I only named the girls. Desdemona and Esme."

He collapsed atop her and laughed so hard, the bed shook.

"I know, I know." She kneed him in the ribs. "I was stupid then. But I'm not a girl anymore."

No, she wasn't.

She was a woman. An accomplished, brave, beautiful woman. An acclaimed authoress. A creative lover.

Best of all, his friend.

And she was laid out before him like a landscape of pristine, snowy hills on a winters' night, lit by a dying ember of sun.

Still holding her hands overhead, he dipped to kiss her brow. Then her nose. Then her lips.

And then down, down. Breasts, belly, navel . . .

She gasped and bucked. "*Dash.*"

He released her arms and settled between her thighs, a man with a purpose. He was not going to get carried away with his own needs this time.

This time, she came first.

"Nora," he whispered, kissing his way back up her body once she'd shuddered and sighed his name.

"Hmm?"

"That word you said, when we locked ourselves outside . . ." He slid a hand beneath her, cupping her arse. "You know, the one a well-bred lady should not know, and most definitely should never speak aloud?"

"Yes." She looked up at him, her eyes drowsy with pleasure. "What of it?"

He flexed his arm and flipped onto his back, bringing her with him. She gave a little shriek of delight.

He tucked her sleek legs on either side of his hips, then propped both hands beneath his head. "I want to hear you say it again."

CHAPTER TEN

Nora woke to the worst sort of knot in her neck, a throbbing twinge her hip, and a dull soreness between her thighs. Her stomach twisted with hunger, tying knots around memories of fried eggs and ham. The fire had gone out, and she was stuck in a bare, humble hut in some unnamed bit of countryside, miles from help or civilization.

But life had never been so wonderful.

She lifted her head from Dash's shoulder. He looked so different in sleep, and not at all like the determined lover who'd transported to bliss her last night.

His chest rose and fell with each easy breath. With the furrows ironed from his forehead, his dark eyebrows couldn't even manage to look severe. He looked peaceful. Content.

At home.

Tenderness welled in her heart. She touched a lock of his dark hair. She didn't know what happened from here, but she had no regrets.

Rising from bed, she pushed on the shutter—just an inch—and glanced out the window. A swatch of blue sky greeted her. It was bright this morning, and clear.

After pulling her shift over her head, she did up her corset in the front, swiveling the laces to the back before cinching them tight. After rolling her dried stockings up her legs and securing them with garters, she stepped into the still-damp wool of her traveling frock, worked her arms through the sleeves, and closed the buttons up to her neck.

Behind her, Dash stirred on the bed.

"Whatever are you doing?" he asked drowsily.

"Making ready." She sat on the stool and laced up her boots. "I expect the driver will be here soon. With luck, I can still make my engagement."

He rubbed his eyes. "You can't still be planning to go to Spindle Cove."

"Of course I am." She twisted her hair into a knot. "Why would you think otherwise?"

"It's impossible. You're not going today. The bridge is out, remember?"

"Oh, drat. Yes, the bridge." Nora sighed. "Well, if it hasn't been repaired, I suppose I'll have no choice but to go back to Canterbury. Can you loan me the money for a private coach? There's always the long way around to Spindle Cove. Perhaps I can just make it."

He struggled up on his elbow. "Nora, don't be absurd. You don't need to go. There's been a storm. They'll understand."

"But what about all those young ladies, waiting to hear me speak?"

He rubbed his eyes. "Waiting to hear you disparage me, you mean."

"Waiting to hear that they're *worth* something. Waiting to hear that their dreams and lives have value, regardless of a man's opinion. It's not about you." She bent to kiss his fore-head. "Perhaps I can't make it, but I want to be ready in case. I'll walk out to the road and fetch a few necessities from my trunk."

He sat up in bed at once. "No, no. I'll fetch it."

"You can't mean to go out like *that*." She smiled.

Lord, he was magnificent by daylight. She gazed at his nakedness, observing the many shades of his body, from sun-bronzed to snowy white. The dark hair on his chest narrowed to an arrow-straight trail bisecting his abdomen.

And at the end of the trail . . .

His manhood stirred. She stood transfixed, watching it swell and stiffen to a ruddy, arcing column of flesh. As if she'd commanded him to rise.

A heady feeling of power suffused her.

She'd done that.

"Come back to bed and join me." He reached out and caught a handful of her skirt.

Oh, no. She whirled away from him with a laugh. They'd never leave at this rate.

Before he could reach her, she was out the door.

The sun was already up, warming the earth. The tree branches dripped overhead, releasing little missiles of water to pierce holes in the crusted blanket of snow.

Her heart lightened. Perhaps the coachman would be on his way soon. This could prove a fine day for traveling.

She made it to the road easily. More difficult, however, was unsecuring her trunk from the carriage's rack. The rain had soaked the knotted rope, and then the sun had shrunk the knots. She pulled off her gloves and attacked them with vigor.

"You must admit," a man said, "that was a bloody good time."

Nora looked up from her struggle with the knots. She spied four gentlemen approaching from the west, walking four horses behind them. Two wore the red coats of officers. As they approached, she could see the other two were dressed in expensive clothes—but they were all looking rather worse for wear.

"You were brilliant with that saber," an officer said to one of the finely dressed men.

"I liked the part where Thorne cracked their heads together."

The handsomest among them flipped the end of his knitted scarf. "And who knew this hideous muffler would make such an effective garrote?"

The one leading the group caught sight of her and stopped in the road. "I don't suppose you're Miss Elinora Browning?"

"Yes," she said, amazed. "Yes, I'm Miss Browning."

"Oh, thank God," said the one with the lethal muffler.

The larger officer only blinked. And loomed, disconcertingly.

"Don't be alarmed," his friend said. "We're harmless. Unless you happen to be part of a smuggling ring."

Nora didn't know what to think.

"Allow us to begin anew. I'm Griffin York, the Duke of Halford. My wife is proprietress of the Two Sisters subscription library in Spindle Cove. She was distressed when the weather turned yesterday and was concerned that you might have been waylaid."

"We're your search party," finished the handsome one.

"Oh," Nora said. "That's wonderful. Our coach skidded off the road. The splinter bar was broken, so the coachman took the horses back to the inn."

"And you stayed in the coach?"

"No, there." She looked toward the tiny herder's hut, just visible through the trees. "But how did you cross the river?"

"The usual way," the duke replied.

"I thought the bridge was out at Rye. Has it already been repaired?"

The men looked from one to another. "I don't recall seeing any damaged bridge, do you?"

His friend shook his head. "None. Not between here and Spindle Cove."

One of the officers examined the carriage hitch. "I thought you said the splinter bar was broken. This looks to be fine to me."

"But that can't be," Nora said. "Unless . . ."

Unless the bridge had never truly been out. And the coach had never truly suffered a broken hitch.

Unless Dash had lied to her. About everything.

Oh, God.

Oh, no.

He *had* to have lied to her. That was the only explanation. Her heart plummeted to her boots. Their entire night together—their lovemaking, their laughter, their friendship—was nothing but a sham?

As the gentlemen began untying her trunk from the top of the coach, Nora stood aside, quietly reeling.

Why, Dash? Why?

Revenge, she supposed. He never wanted her to reach

Spindle Cove. If she failed to appear, she wouldn't be able to speak against him. Then word would spread quickly, questions would be asked. Soon everyone would know that she'd been compromised. Humiliated. Discredited. Her image as a bastion of defiant spinsterhood would be destroyed. He would be free to pursue his career. His plans to marry. Unencumbered by Nora.

The bastard.

The smug, cunning, seducing bastard.

Nora still had time. She could outrun the prospect of ruin, with luck. So long as she arrived in Spindle Cove for her reading today, no one would ever be the wiser.

"I don't suppose we could use the coach?" she asked the duke hopefully.

He shook his head. "We haven't the right tackle or horses, I'm afraid. But if you can ride with me, we'll just make it."

She looked at the horse, her stomach turning. Inside her chest, her fear did furious battle with her anger. Could she manage it?

"*Nora!*"

The deep call rang out from the direction of the herder's hut.

She clenched her jaw.

"Nora!" Dash had pulled on his clothing and started to walk toward the road. He cupped his hands around his mouth and called again. "Nora!"

"Who's that man?" the duke asked.

"No one important," Nora replied.

"He seems to know you."

"He's a fellow traveler. He helped me find shelter last

night. But he was highly unpleasant and presumptuous. I'm glad to be quit of him, truth be told."

She went to the duke's horse and mustered all her courage before accepting his help in mounting the beast. As she settled sideways on the saddle, her stomach skipped about her chest.

"Nora, wait!" Dash had started running now, charging across the fields with his shirt collar open and his trousers held up with one hand. "Don't leave! I can explain everything."

So, he admitted it was all a ruse.

The shameless rogue. The liar.

"Do you want us to thrash him for you?" the duke offered. "We're rather good at it, thrashing blackguards."

The other men nodded in agreement.

"We've a sort of gang," the handsome one said. "Legendary in these parts. You might have heard of us. Lords of Perdition."

The largest—Captain Thorne, was it?—cracked his neck in an ominous way.

"That's tempting," she said, imagining Dash's neck constricted by an ugly striped muffler. *Very, very tempting.* "But no. Let's just be off."

The duke mounted behind her. As the horse kicked into a canter, Nora held tight to the pommel and blinked a stupid tear from her eye. She would not cry. Instead, she took comfort in the same knowledge that had steadied her once before:

Lord Dashwood had missed out.

Again.

And this time, Nora wouldn't look back.

The day looked a good deal brighter than Pauline felt.

She and Daniela had gone about the morning as if all were fine and going as planned, partly to keep Daniela happy and partly because Pauline didn't know what else to do with herself.

She was worried about Miss Browning. The author in question had as yet failed to appear.

But most of all, she was worried for Griff.

Charlotte Highwood breezed through the library's front door, drawing at once to Pauline's side and putting an arm about her shoulders. "Do cease making fretful faces, Your Grace. You'll smudge the windowpane."

"Your mother decided to let you attend?" Pauline asked. "Or did you come without her approval?"

"She sent me over. There was never any question." Charlotte plucked a volume from the shelf of new arrivals and cracked the spine. "This is Spindle Cove. Mama always says, you never know when a wealthy, handsome gentleman might appear."

Something out the window caught Pauline's eye. "Your mother might be more clever than we give her credit for."

Because not one, but *four* such gentleman appeared at that moment, emerging over the distant rise like legends. Heroes, come home from war. Walking their horses behind them and passing a flask from one to another.

Griff.

She dashed out the door, not caring about the puddles that muddied her boots and hem. She scarcely even saw the other three men. Her eyes were for her husband alone.

She ran to him and flung her arms around his neck. The greeting wasn't very duchessly, perhaps, but it was entirely sincere. His arms came around her tight.

Nothing else mattered but this.

When she managed to pull back, Pauline noticed that her husband was wearing an appalling amount of mud, and one or two fresh rents in his clothing—in addition to his boyish grin.

And on his cheek, was that . . . blood?

"Sorry we're late," he said, eyes gleaming with mischief. "It took us some time to find her, what with the storm."

"But you did find her?"

"Of course. I promised she'd be here in time." He looked over his shoulder.

It was only then that Pauline noticed a pale, blue-clad young lady perched on his gelding. Lord Payne helped her to dismount. Miss Browning looked extremely happy to be reacquainted with solid ground.

Her husband said, "Miss Browning, may I present your hostess. My wife, Her Grace, the Duchess of Halford."

Miss Browning dropped in a deep curtsy. Pauline inclined her head in greeting, as it befit a woman of her wedded rank to do. She didn't know if she would ever get used to this, but for Griff and her children's sake, she tried.

"Miss Browning," she said. "I'm so delighted to see you here."

"I am delighted to be here." She cast a look about their surroundings. "I wonder, is there some place where I might wash up? And a bite to eat would be most welcome. It's been quite a journey."

"Yes, of course."

Colin and Charlotte escorted her guest to the Queen's Ruby inn, and Lord Bramwell and Captain Thorne expressed their desire to retreat to the Bull and Blossom for a hearty breakfast.

Pauline and her husband were left alone.

"I'm so sorr—"

"About yesterd—"

They both spoke at once, and then they both laughed. Griff made a *ladies-first* motion.

"I'm so sorry about yesterday. That was hardly the welcome home you deserved. The sherry didn't matter. I don't want to be one of those nagging wives who demands a complete accounting of her husband's every step."

"It was my fault for being so forgetful. And secretive. But can you blame me?" He took a glance at the snow-capped church steeple. "It *is* nearly Christmas, Pauline."

From his pocket, he withdrew a slender oval on a gold chain and pressed it into her hand.

"A locket?" She pried open the tiny clasp, and inside was a miniature. "Oh, it's you."

He made a self-effacing grimace. "I've been searching London for a decent portrait painter. This seemed the best way to get a sample of his work."

Portraits. They weren't something that Pauline had really thought to have. For girls who grew up in homes like hers, portraits were unimaginable luxuries. She made memories instead.

She looked up into her husband's face, gazing on those strong, handsome features preserved in her memory and etched on her heart, down to each faint laugh line and whisker of shadow.

"I meant to surprise you at Christmas," he said. "Mostly so we could arrange a proper portrait of the children. But I hoped perhaps you'd want this one, too. You know, so long as it was already made." He sounded a touch uncertain. "I know it's not perfect. We were pressed for time. My forehead can't possibly be that big, and—"

"It's wonderful." She closed the locket and held it tight in her hand, until she felt its shape imprinted on her palm. "I love it."

And I love you. Love you, love you. With all my heart.

"Good. Then I hope you'll give me a present in return."

"Oh?"

"I want you to sit for a portrait, too."

She started to object. "But surely that's not necessary. Unlike you and the children, I'm not in the noble line. And I'm not really a portrait sort of lady."

"I don't give a damn about posterity. This is me we're discussing, and you know I'm entirely selfish. I want this for myself. The past three weeks have been a trial." He touched her lips. "I miss you like hell when we're apart."

"I missed you, too."

"And if you need any extra convincing, did I mention I found you some very fine sherry just off the ship from Spain?"

"You did? How on earth did you manage that?"

"Found a little country spot. Open late."

With a slight smile, she relented. "Very well, then."

"You'll sit for a portrait?"

As if she could she deny him anything. "Yes."

He rested his forehead to hers. "Good."

She whispered coyly, "With clothing, or without?"

CHAPTER ELEVEN

Later that afternoon, cleaned up and freshly coiffed, Nora read aloud to an audience of dozens in the Two Sisters subscription library. Ladies, mostly. But the gentlemen who'd come to her aid that morning lined the wall, as well.

She could think of no more perfect occasion to refresh her memory of these words. If she could, she would sit down and write them all again.

"{dec63}As the new day dawns, and my inkwell runs dry, I hereby make a vow. Not a vow to the man I once hoped to marry, but a promise to myself. From this morning forward, I will never shed another tear for him. There is no need. Because everything Lord Da—'" She cleared her throat, then began again. "{dec63}Everything Lord *Ashwood* rejected when he so callously walked away—is mine to claim. Mine to use. My wit, my strength, and most of all—my heart. I will not put any of these on the shelf.'"

There was a moment of silence. Then polite applause rippled through the crowded subscription library.

The duchess moved forward. "Thank you so much for that

reading, Miss Browning. We have sherry and teacakes for everyone, and Miss Browning has agreed to sign copies of her work. But first, are there any questions?"

"I have a question." The male voice came from somewhere in the back row. Near the entrance.

Her pulse stuttered.

Dash.

He jostled into view. All six broad-shouldered, darkly handsome feet of him.

She averted her eyes before she could drink him in any further.

He repeated, "I have a question, Nora."

"Just who the devil *are* you?" the duke asked.

"I'm George Travers, Lord Dashwood."

With a little squeal of excitement, Charlotte Highwood lifted her copy of the pamphlet. "Do you he's mean *the* Lord—"

"No," Nora snapped. "Dashwood, not Ashwood. The pamphlet isn't about him."

Charlotte's shoulders fell. "Well, that seems a great coincidence."

"Precisely my thoughts on the matter," Dash agreed.

Nora spoke through clenched teeth. "You have a great deal of nerve, coming here."

The crowd bustled with excitement. Whispers chased from one set of lips to the next: *It is him. It must be.*

"I must speak with you," he said.

"Why? So you can tell me more falsehoods?"

"No, I—"

"You lied to me," she bit out. "About the road, the coach,

the bridge. Everything." She skewered him with a glare. "I'll bet you weren't even a virgin."

The bustling of the crowd abruptly ceased. One could have heard a snowflake twirl to the floor.

Lord Payne tossed back a swallow of sherry. "I really must attend these things more often."

Dash cleared his throat. "Yes, I lied. About a few things. Not everything. But I did pay off the coachman. Well, both coachmen. And the innkeeper in Canterbury."

Her jaw dropped. "*You're* the reason the first coach left without me."

"Yes. And the bridge was never out, and the hitch was fine. You're right. I lied. I'm sorry for the deceit, but I was desperate for time alone with you, and I knew you'd never agree. I needed to know if I had any chance."

"Any chance at what?"

"At convincing you to marry me."

Now every woman in the library gasped in shock.

Nora could only conclude their collective gasp had sucked all the air out of the room—because she could no longer breathe at all.

Dash threaded his way through the rows of chairs, came to stand before her, and went down on one knee.

"Stop," she told him, finding her voice.

"No."

"Go away."

"Marry me."

"Do get up," she pleaded.

He gave her a teasing look. "Say yes first."

"I won't agree to this. I can't."

"You can, and you should. We'll be perfectly not-perfect together. If we can just stop fighting ourselves long enough to be wed."

"How can you say that? You mistreated me, abandoned me, used me, and deceived me."

"I also carried you, kissed you, warmed you, and gave you pleasure." In a devilish murmur, he added, "Twice."

Her face heated. "You can't even propose to me without being infuriating. What makes you think I'd even consider marrying you now?"

"Because you're remarkable, Nora." He reached for her hand and held it in both of his. "And every brave, brilliant accomplishment in your life began as something you did to spite me."

The truth of his words sank into her bones. He was right. Beginning with their lessons as children, continuing with the pamphlet and her speaking career . . . not to mention, everything they'd done last night. Even riding away from the cottage this morning—on horseback, for the first time in years.

In every instance, she'd wanted to get the better of Dash. And she'd ended up making something better of herself.

"If that's the case," she said, "then I should continue to spite you."

"And what better way to keep me within spiting distance, than to marry me and spend life at my side?"

Oh, he was impossible. Nora didn't know what to say to that.

"This is what you wanted," he said. "What you still want, in your heart. And it's what I've wanted, too."

Now *that* irked her. He'd gone too far with that claim.

"You never wanted this. You want a convenient bride, and you want to soothe your pride. That's all. In all these years, you never thought of me."

"You're so wrong. I've wanted this. I came back to England solely with the intention of courting you. I thought of you all the time. Every day I was away." His Adam's apple bobbed in his unshaven throat. "Every night."

"No. You're only saying so now."

"I'm not. It's true."

"There's nothing in the world that could convince me of that."

"My darling Nora. The world is exactly what will prove it." Rising to his feet, he turned to Pauline where she stood behind the counter. "Fetch me a copy of *Sir Bertram Coddington's World Atlas*, if you would. The newest edition."

The duchess said, "I don't have a copy of *Sir Bertram Coddington's World Atlas*. In any edition."

"Is this not a bookshop?"

"No. It's a subscription library of books selected to interest young ladies on seaside holiday."

The Duke of Halford glowered at him. "And unless you want to become intimately acquainted with our local waters—by way of the nearest cliff—I suggest you address my wife as 'Your Grace.'"

Dash quickly recovered his manners, inclining his head in a bow. "I beg your pardon, Your Grace."

"My father has a copy of that atlas at Summerfield, I believe," said Lady Rycliff. Nora had taken an instant liking to her when they met. Ginger-haired, freckled ladies needed to band together.

"Then do let's go to Summerfield," Dash replied.

"I'm not leaving here," Nora protested. "I have a lecture to give."

"You just finished that. You were on to questions."

"Then I have questions to answer." She looked around and nodded at a round-faced girl who'd raised her hand. "Go ahead, dear. What was your question?"

The round-faced girl looked at Dash. "What's in the atlas?"

Nora sighed.

He grinned. "Perhaps someone else can fetch the book."

She looked toward the gentlemen who'd made up her search party. "They're not going to help you. None of them will help you."

"Charlotte will fetch it," Mrs. Highwood declared.

"I will?" Charlotte asked.

"Yes." The matron nudged her daughter's side and whispered loudly, "Can't you see? The spinster is going to refuse him, and then he'll be on the market again. I know he's only a baron, but he is a handsome and wealthy one. This is your chance to be first in line."

"Oh, Mama." Charlotte covered her face.

"I'll go with you, Charlotte," Lady Rycliff volunteered. "It's my father's house, and I'll admit—my curiosity's piqued, too."

Once they'd departed, Dash gestured in invitation. "Go on with your talk, if you like."

Nora sighed. How could she, with him standing there? She would wait for his atlas, and then she would be done with him.

In the meantime, she sat down, poured herself an inch of sherry, and downed it in one swallow.

Time had never passed so slowly. Nora tapped her boot heel against the chair leg. The assembled ladies sat staring and whispering among themselves. Their hostess passed around teacakes.

For his part, Dash merely stood a few feet away, hat in hand, gazing at Nora. Boldly. Unabashedly. Even, she fancied, adoringly.

"Do you know," he said, "you're ravishing when you're trying to hate me forever."

She couldn't even look at him. "This ends today. When she returns with that atlas, you're leaving."

"When she returns with that atlas, you're going to be overwhelmed. You might even cry."

"I will not. You're mad."

He smiled. "Yes. But only a little, and entirely for you."

Another several minutes passed. "It doesn't matter what's in that atlas. I couldn't marry you. I've spent years telling young ladies that their value isn't bound up in their marital status. What message would I send if I abandoned my career to marry you and bear your children?"

"To begin, there is no better way to prove the worth of one's mind than to display a willingness to change it. Secondly, who said anything about abandoning your career? I'd never ask it. I believe it's possible to write on board a ship."

On board a ship?

She turned to look at him. "You'd take me with you?"

"If you wish to go. And I suspect you do, if only to castigate me on other continents. There's an idea. Come with me

to Tahiti and insult me on a white sand beach. Berate me on
a South American mountaintop—so loudly, the echo sets off
an avalanche."

Despite all her intentions to dampen it, a flame of excitement kindled in her heart.

And then he threw a log on the fire. "Aside from a thrilling
honeymoon, you must admit it would make quite a book."

Curse the man. He understood exactly how to tempt her.

"Just imagine the memoir. You could call it *Lord Ashwood's Ship Has Sailed*. I'm certain the reading public would
be fascinated."

Several of the women in attendance nodded eagerly.

"Here it is!" Charlotte came dashing through the door,
breathless. She plunked the immense volume down on the
counter. "Lud. It weighs as much as a small mule."

"Do you often carry small mules?" Dash asked her.

"Oh no, my lord. She does not," Mrs. Highwood inter-
jected, sidling up to Dash with a coquettish giggle. "My
Charlotte is accomplished in all the feminine arts. Music,
sketching, dancing, embroidery . . ."

"*Mama.*"

Charlotte yanked her mother away by force, leaving Nora
and Dash with the atlas. Young ladies rose from their seats
and gathered round.

Dash opened it, flipping through the plates before opening the volume to a detailed map of Upper Canada.

"Look." He pointed to a miniscule oval on the map, with
a bit of barely decipherable lettering next to it. "Read that.
What does it say?"

"'Nora Pond,'" she read aloud, squinting. "So that's it? I'm

supposed to agree to marry you because you named a pond
for me in Upper Canada?"

"No, no. The pond doesn't exist."

She stared at him.

"Most land features are named already," he explained,
"and for those that aren't, Sir Bertram has a miles-long list
of patrons and royalty to whom he's promised landmarks. I
don't get to decide on much of anything, in terms of reality.
But we put a deliberately false feature in every map, you see.
That way, we can tell if they've been copied. And these, I'm
permitted to name."

"So you named *nothing* after me."

"Not just the once." He flipped through the pages of the
atlas, pausing on each spread to point out some notch or pin-
prick. "Here's Mount Browning, you see. A total fiction. And
Nora Creek on this one, also false. Ah, here we have Elinora
Point."

"You named *several* nothings after me."

"Yes," he said, excitedly. "Do you understand now?"

"No. I don't."

He shoved the atlas aside and took her face in his hands.
"I named all the nothings after you. Because, my darling
Nora . . . no matter where I traveled, you were always what
was missing."

"Oh."

Her eyes burned at the corners.

Drat him. She was *not* going to cry.

She swallowed hard. She blinked. She tried to divert her
mind to trivial, unpleasant things. Like tangled stockings, or
raspberry seeds, or . . .

But his eyes. There wasn't any escaping the rich, midnight darkness of his eyes—nor the affection she saw within them.

Her heart overflowed.

His thumb swiped at her cheek. "See. I told you you'd cry."

She sniffed. "I despise you."

"No, you don't." He smiled. "Not any more than I despise you. Trust me, I know how it stings when someone tells you the truth about yourself. It's like catching a glimpse of your reflection in a looking glass when you're not prepared. Intolerable. I *was* furious when I read your pamphlet—but only because I knew it was the truth. I'd known it for some time. The reality set in somewhere around the Tropic of Capricorn. When I left you behind at Greenwillow Hall . . . I'd missed out."

"Then you should have turned back."

"It was too late for that." He kissed her lips. "Luckily, the world is a sphere. I was always traveling toward you. I just took the long way around."

"For a map-maker, you're shockingly bad with directions."

He shrugged in admission. "Then you'd best stay close. So I don't lose the way."

They stood that way for a long moment, just staring into each other's eyes.

Really? she asked him without words.

He nodded. *Really.*

"I love you," he murmured. "You rode away before I could say it this morning, but I love every part of you, Elinora Jane Browning. Mind, body, soul. Send me away if you like. I'll honor your wishes. But this heart will always be yours."

"I'm confused," Mrs. Highwood moaned from somewhere nearby. "What are my Charlotte's chances? Is the handsome, wealthy baron still single or not?"

Without turning his gaze from Nora, Dash lifted an eyebrow. "Care to answer?"

"This handsome, wealthy baron is not single. Not any longer." Nora smiled. "Lord Dashwood has met his match."

He gathered her to him and kissed her soundly. Everything around them melted away. There was only the heat of sherry and the sweetness of teacakes and the delicious spice of the passion between them.

Blended together, it tasted like victory. A triumph they could share, and savor for a lifetime.

Applause greeted them when they parted at last.

Except from one quarter of the room, where a displeased matron flicked open her fan. "Don't worry, Charlotte. There's still the Ashwood one, then."

A Note from the Author

Thank you so much for reading! I hope you enjoyed *Lord Dashwood Missed Out*. If you feel so inclined, I invite you to recommend this book to a friend or post an honest review. Recommendations and reviews help other readers find new books to enjoy.

If you're new to Spindle Cove, here's the full series in suggested reading order:

A Night to Surrender (Susanna and Bram, Book One)

Once Upon a Winter's Eve (Violet and Christian, novella)

A Week to be Wicked (Minerva and Colin, Book Two)

A Lady by Midnight (Kate and Thorne, Book Three)

Beauty and the Blacksmith (Diana and Aaron, novella)

Any Duchess Will Do (Pauline and Griff, Book Four)

And coming in 2016, look for Spindle Cove, Book Five:

Do You Want to Start a Scandal, where the youngest of the Highwood sisters, Charlotte, finally gets her hero!

The best way to receive updates about Charlotte's story and my other new books is to sign up for my email newsletter at: tessadare.com/newsletter-signup.

You can also visit my website, www.TessaDare.com, for all the most current information.

Keep reading for an excerpt from of my latest bestseller, *When a Scot Ties the Knot!*

Tessa

Keep reading for an excerpt from RITA® Award winner
Tessa Dare's *New York Times* bestseller

WHEN A SCOT TIES THE KNOT

On the cusp of her first London season, Miss Madeline
Gracechurch was shy, pretty and talented with a drawing
pencil, but hopelessly awkward with gentlemen. She was
certain to be a dismal failure on the London marriage
mart. So Maddie did what generations of shy, awkward
young ladies have done: she invented a sweetheart.

A Scottish sweetheart. One who was handsome and
honorable and devoted to her, but conveniently never
around. Maddie poured her heart into writing the
imaginary Captain MacKenzie letter after letter . . . and
by pretending to be devastated when he was (not really)
killed in battle, she managed to avoid the pressures of
London society entirely.

Until years later, when this kilted Highland lover of
her imaginings shows up in the flesh. The real Captain
Logan MacKenzie arrives on her doorstep—handsome
as anything, but not entirely honorable. He's wounded,
jaded, in possession of her letters . . . and ready to make
good on every promise Maddie never expected to keep.

Available now!

CHAPTER ONE

Invernesshire, Scotland
April 1817

*B*lub.

Blub-blub-blub.

Maddie's hand jerked.

Ink sputtered from her pen, making great blots on the
wing structure she'd been outlining. Her delicate Brazilian
dragonfly now resembled a leprous chicken.

Two hours of work, gone in a heartbeat.

But it would be nothing if those bubbles signified what
she hoped.

Copulation.

Her heart began to beat faster. She set aside her pen,
lifted her head just enough for a clear view of the glass-walled
seawater tank, and went still.

Maddie was, by nature, an observer. She knew how to
fade into the background, be it drawing-room wallpaper,

ballroom wainscoting, or the plastered-over stone of Lannair Castle. And she had a great deal of experience observing the mating rituals of many strange and wondrous creatures, from English aristocrats to cabbage moths.

When it came to courtship, however, lobsters were the most prudish and formal of all.

She'd been waiting months for Fluffy, the female, to molt and declare herself available to mate. So had Rex, the male specimen in the tank. She didn't know which of them was the more frustrated.

Perhaps today would be the day. Maddie peered hard at the tank, breathless with anticipation.

There. From behind a broken chunk of coral, a slender orange antennae waved in the murky gloom.

Hallelujah.

That's it, she silently willed. *Go on, Fluffy. That's a girl. It's been a long, lonely winter under that rock. But you're ready now.*

A blue claw appeared.

Then receded.

Shameless tease.

"Stop being so missish."

At last, the female's full head came into view as she rose from her hiding place.

And then someone rapped at the door. "Miss Grace-church?"

That was the end of that.

With a *blub-blub-blub,* Fluffy disappeared as quickly as she'd emerged. Back under her rock.

Drat.

"What is it, Becky?" Maddie called. "Is my aunt ill?"

If she'd been disturbed in her studio, *someone* must be ill. The servants knew not to interrupt her when she was working.

"No one's ill, miss. But there's a caller for you."

"A caller? Now that's a surprise."

For an on-the-shelf Englishwoman residing in the barren wilds of the Scottish Highlands, callers were always a surprise.

"Who is it?" she asked.

"It's a man."

A *man.*

Now Maddie was more than surprised. She was positively shocked.

She pushed aside her ruined dragonfly illustration and stood to peer out the window. No luck. She'd chosen this tower room for its breathtaking view of the rugged green hills and the glassy loch settled like a mirror shard between them. It offered no useful vantage of the gate or entryway.

"Oh, Miss Gracechurch." Becky sounded nervous. "He's ever so big."

"Goodness. And does this big man have a name?"

"No. I mean, he must *have* a name, mustn't he? But he didn't say. Not yet. Your aunt thought you had best come and see for yourself."

Well. This grew more and more mysterious.

"I'll be there in a moment. Ask Cook to prepare some tea, if you will."

Maddie untied her smock. After pulling the apron over her head and hanging it on a nearby peg, she took a quick inventory of her appearance. Her slate-gray frock wasn't too wrinkled, but her hands were stained with ink and her hair was a travesty—loose and disheveled. There was no time for a proper coiffure. No hairpins to be found, either. She gathered the dark locks in her hands and twisted them into a loose knot at the back of her head, securing the chignon with a nearby pencil. The best she could do under the circumstances.

Whoever this unexpected, nameless, ever-so-big man was, he wasn't likely to be impressed with her.

But then, men seldom were.

She took her time descending the spiraling stairs, wondering who this visitor might be. Most likely a land agent from a neighboring estate. Lord Varleigh wasn't due until tomorrow, and Becky would have known his name.

When Maddie finally reached the bottom, Aunt Thea joined her.

Her aunt touched a hand to her turban with dramatic flair. "Oh, Madling. At last."

"Where is our mysterious caller? In the hall?"

"The parlor." Her aunt took her arm, and together they moved down the corridor. "Now, my dear. You must be calm."

"I *am* calm. Or at least, I *was* calm until you said that." She studied her aunt's face for clues. "What on earth is going on?"

"There may be a shock. But don't you worry. Once it's over, I'll make a posset to set you straight."

A posset.

Oh, dear. Aunt Thea fancied herself something of an amateur apothecary. The trouble was, her "cures" were usually worse than the disease.

"It's only a caller. I'm sure a posset won't be necessary."

Maddie resolved to maintain squared shoulders and an air of good health when she greeted this big, nameless man.

When they stepped into the parlor, her resolve was tested.

This wasn't just a man.

This was a *man*.

A tall, commanding figure of a Scotsman, dressed in what appeared to be military uniform: a kilt of dark green-and-blue plaid, paired with the traditional redcoat.

His hair was overlong (mostly brown, with hints of ginger), and his squared jaw sported several days' growth of whiskers (mostly ginger, with hints of brown). Broad shoulders tapered to a trim torso. A simple black sporran was slung low around his waist, and a sheathed dirk rode his hip. Below the fall of his kilt, muscled, hairy legs disappeared into white hose and scuffed black boots.

Maddie pleaded with herself not to stare.

It was a losing campaign.

Taken altogether, his appearance was a veritable assault of virility.

"Good afternoon." She managed an awkward curtsy.

He did not answer or bow. Wordlessly, he approached her.

And at the point where a well-mannered gentleman would stop, he drew closer still.

She shifted her weight from one foot to the other, anxious. At least he'd solved her staring problem. She could scarcely bear to look at him now.

He stopped close enough for Maddie to breathe in the scents of whisky and wood smoke, and to glimpse a wide, devilish mouth slashing through his light growth of beard. After long seconds, she coaxed herself into meeting his gaze.

His eyes were a breathtaking blue. And not in a good way. They were the sort of blue that gave one the feeling of being launched into the sky or plunged into icy water. Flung into a void with no hope of return. It wasn't a pleasant sensation.

"Miss Madeline Gracechurch?"

Oh, his voice was the worst part of all. Deep, with that Highland burr that scraped and hollowed words out, forcing them to hold more meaning.

She nodded.

He said, "I'm come home to you."

"H-home . . . to *me*?"

"I knew it," Aunt Thea said. "It's him."

The strange man nodded. "It's me."

"It's who?" Maddie blurted out.

She didn't mean to be rude, but she'd never laid eyes on this man in her life. She was quite sure of it. His wasn't a face or figure she'd be likely to forget. He made quite an impression. More than an impression. She felt flattened by him.

"Don't you know me, *mo chridhe*?"

She shook her head. She'd had enough of this game, thank you. "Tell me your name."

The corner of his mouth tipped in a small, roguish smile. "Captain Logan MacKenzie."

No.

The world became a violent swirl of colors: green and red and that stark, dangerous blue.

"Did you . . ." Maddie faltered. "Surely you didn't say Cap—"

That was as far as she got. Her tongue gave up.

And then her knees gave out.

She didn't swoon or crumple. She simply sat down, hard.

Her backside hit the settee, and the air was forced from her lungs. "*Oof.*"

The Scotsman stared down at her, looking faintly amused. "Are ye well?"

"No," she said honestly. "I'm seeing things. This can't be happening."

This really, truly, could *not* be happening.

Captain Logan MacKenzie could not be alive. He could not be dead, either.

He didn't exist.

To be sure, for nigh on a decade now, everyone had believed her to be first pining after, then mourning for, the man who was nothing but fiction.

Maddie had spent countless afternoons writing him letters—missives that had actually just been pages of nonsense or sketches of moths and snails. She'd declined to attend parties and balls, citing her devotion to the Highland hero of her dreams—but really because she'd preferred to stay home with a book.

Her godfather, the Earl of Lynforth, had even left her Lannair Castle in his will so that she might be nearer her beloved's home. Quite thoughtful of the old dear.

And when the deceit began to weigh on her conscience, Maddie had given her Scottish officer a brave, honorable, and entirely fictional death. She'd worn black for a full year, then gray thereafter. Everyone believed her to be disconsolate, but black and gray suited her. They hid the smudges of ink and charcoal that came from her work.

Thanks to Captain MacKenzie, she had a home, an income, work she enjoyed—and no pressure to move in

London society. She'd never intended to deceive her family for so many years, but no one had been hurt. It all seemed to have worked for the best.

Until now.

Now something had gone terribly wrong.

Maddie turned her head by slow degrees, Miss Muffet fashion, forcing herself to look at the Highlander who'd sat down beside her. Her heart thumped in her chest.

If her Captain MacKenzie didn't exist, who was this man? And what did he want from her?

"You aren't real." She briefly closed her eyes and pinched herself, hoping to waken from this horrid dream. "You. Aren't. Real."

Aunt Thea pressed a hand to her throat. With the other, she fanned herself vigorously. "Surely it must be a miracle. To think, we were told you were—"

"Dead?" The officer's gaze never left Maddie's. A hint of irony sharpened his voice. "I'm not dead. Touch and see for yourself."

Touch?

Oh, no. Touching him was out of the question. There would not be any touching.

But before Maddie knew what was happening, he'd caught her ungloved hand and drawn it inside his unbuttoned coat, pressing it to his chest.

And they were touching.

Intimately.

A stupid, instinctive thrill shot through her. She'd never held hands with any man. Never felt a man's skin pressed against her own. Curiosity clamored louder than her objections.

His hand was large and strong. Roughened with calluses, marked with scars and powder burns. Those marks revealed his life to be one of battle and strife, just as surely as her pale, ink-stained fingers told hers to be a life of scribbling . . . and no adventure at all.

He flattened her palm against the well-worn lawn of his shirt. Beneath it, he was impressively solid. Warm.

Real.

"I'm no ghost, *mo chridhe*. Just a man. Flesh and bone."

Mo chridhe.

He kept using those words. She wasn't fluent in Gaelic, but over the years she'd gathered a few bits here and there. She knew *mo chridhe* meant "my heart."

The words were a lover's endearment, but there was no tenderness in his voice. Only a low, simmering anger. He spoke the words like a man who'd cut out his own heart long ago and left it buried in the cold, dark ground.

With their joined hands, he eased aside one lapel of his coat. The gesture revealed a corner of yellowed paper tucked inside his breast pocket. She recognized the handwriting on the envelope.

It was her own.

"I received your letters, lass. Every last one."

God help her. He knew.

He knew she'd lied. He knew everything.

And he was here to make her pay.

"Aunt Thea," she whispered, "I believe I'll be needing that posset after all."

So, Logan thought. *This is the girl.*

At last he had her in his grasp. Madeline Eloise Grace-church. In her own words, the greatest ninny to ever draw breath in England.

The lass wasn't in England now. And pale as she'd grown in the past few seconds, he suspected she might not be breathing, either.

He gave her hand a little squeeze, and she drew in a gasp. Color flooded her cheeks.

There, that was better.

To be truthful, Logan needed a moment to locate his own composure. She'd knocked the breath from him, too.

He'd spent a great deal of time wondering how she looked. Too much time over the years. Of course she'd sent him sketches of every blessed mushroom, moth, and blossom in existence—but never any likenesses of herself.

By the gods, she was bonny. Far prettier than her letters had led him to imagine. Also smaller, more delicate.

"So . . ." she said, "this means . . . you . . . I . . . gack."

Much less articulate, too.

Logan's gaze slid to her aunt, who was somehow *exactly* as he'd always pictured her. Frail shoulders, busy eyes, saffron-yellow turban.

"Perhaps you'll permit us a few minutes alone, Aunt Thea. May I call you Aunt Thea?"

"But . . . certainly you may."

"No," his betrothed moaned. "Please, don't."

Logan patted her slender shoulder. "There, there."

Aunt Thea hurried to excuse her niece. "You must forgive her, Captain. We believed you dead for years. She's worn mourning ever since. To have you back again . . . well, it's such a shock. She's overwrought."

"That's understandable," he said.

And it was.

Logan would be surprised, too, if a person he'd invented from thin air, then cravenly lied about for close to a decade, appeared on his doorstep one afternoon.

Surprised, shocked . . . perhaps even frightened.

Madeline Gracechurch appeared to be no less than terrified.

"What was it you mentioned wanting, *mo chridhe*? A poultice?"

"A posset," Aunt Thea said. "I'll heat one at once."

As soon as her aunt had left the room, Logan tightened his grip around Madeline's slender wrist, drawing her to her feet.

The motion seemed to help her find her tongue.

"Who are you?" she whispered.

"I thought we covered that already."

"Have you no conscience, coming in here as an imposter and frightening my aunt?"

"Imposter?" He made an amused sound. "I'm no imposter, lass. But I'll admit—I am entirely without conscience."

She wet her lips with a nervous flick of her tongue, drawing his gaze to a small, kiss-shaped mouth that might otherwise have escaped his attention.

Wondering what else he might have missed, he let his eyes wander down her figure, from the untidy knot of dark hair atop her head to . . . whatever sort of body might be hiding under that high-necked gray shroud.

It didn't matter, he told himself. He hadn't come for the carnal attractions.

He was here to collect what he was owed.

Logan inhaled deep. The air hovering about her carried a familiar scent.

When you smell lavender, victory is near.

Her hand went to her brow. "I can't understand what's happening."

"Can't you? Is it so hard to believe that the name and rank you plucked from the air might belong to an actual man somewhere? MacKenzie's not an uncommon name. The British Army's a vast pool of candidates."

"Yes, but I never properly addressed anything. I specifically wrote the number of a regiment that doesn't exist. Never indicated any location. I just tossed them into the post."

"Well, somehow—"

"Somehow they found their way to you." She swallowed audibly. "And you . . . Oh, no. And you *read* them?"

He opened his mouth to reply.

"Of course you read them," she said, cutting him off. "You couldn't be here if you hadn't."

Logan didn't know whether to be annoyed or grateful that she kept completing his side of the conversation. He supposed it was habit on her part. She'd conducted a one-sided correspondence with him for years.

And then, once he'd served his purpose, she'd had the nerve to kill him off.

This canny little English heiress thought she'd come up with the perfect scheme to avoid being pressured into marriage.

She was about to learn she'd been wrong.

Verra wrong.

"Oh, dear," she muttered. "I think I'll be sick."

"I must say, this is a fine welcome home."

"This isn't your home."

It will be, lass. It will be.

Logan decided to give her a moment to compose herself. He made a slow circle of the room. The castle itself was remarkable. A classic fortified tower house, kept in a fair state of repair. This chamber they currently occupied was hung with ancient tapestries but was otherwise furnished in what he assumed to be typical English style.

But he didn't care about carpets and settees.

He paused at the window. It was the surrounding land that interested him. This glen was ideal. A wide, green ribbon of fertile land stretched alongside the clear loch. Beyond it lay open hills for grazing.

These were the Highlands his soldiers had known in their youths. The Highlands that had all but disappeared by the time they'd returned from war. Stolen by greedy English landlords—and the occasional fanciful spinster.

This would be home for them now. Here, in the shadow of Lannair Castle, his men could regain what had been taken from them. There was space enough in this glen to raise cottages, plant crops, start families.

Rebuild a life.

Logan would stop at nothing to give them that chance. He owed his men that much. He owed them far more.

"You," she announced, "have to leave."

"Leave? Not a chance, *mo chridhe*."

"You have to leave. Now."

She took him by the sleeve and tried tugging him toward the door. Unsuccessfully.

Then she gave up on the tugging and started pushing at him instead.

That wasn't any help, either. Except, perhaps, as an aid to Logan's amusement.

He was a lot of man, and she was a mere slip of a lass. He couldn't help but laugh. But her efforts weren't entirely ineffectual. The press of her tiny hands on his arms and chest stirred him in dangerous places.

He'd gone a long time without a woman's touch.

Far too long.

At length, she gave up on the pulling and pushing, and went straight to her last resort.

Pleading. Big, brown calf's eyes implored him for mercy. Little did she know, this was the least likely tactic to work. Logan wasn't a man to be moved by tender emotion.

However, he was a man—and he wasn't unmoved by a pretty face. What with all her exertions, he was starting to see a flush of color on her cheeks. And an intriguing spark of mystery behind those wide, dark eyes.

This lass didn't belong in gray. With that dark hair and those rosy lips, she belonged in vibrant color. Deep Highland greens or sapphire blue.

His own smile took him by surprise.

She was going to look bonny wearing his plaid.

"Just go," she said. "If you leave now, I can convince my aunt this was all a mistake. Because it *was* a mistake. You must know that. I never meant to bother you with my silly ramblings."

"Perhaps you didna mean to. But involve me you did."

"Is it an apology you want, then? I'm sorry. So very, very sorry. Please, if you'll just give me the letters back and be on your way, I'll be most generous. I'd be glad to pay you for your troubles."

Logan shook his head. She thought a bribe would appease him? "I'm not leaving, lass. Not for all the pin money in your wee silk reticule."

"Then what *do* you want?"

"That's simple. I want what your letters said. What you've been telling your family for years. I'm Captain Logan MacKenzie. I received every last one of your missives, and despite your best attempts to kill me, I am verra much alive."

He propped a finger under her chin, tilting her face to his. So she would be certain to hear and believe his words.

"Madeline Eloise Gracechurch . . . I've come here to marry you."

ABOUT THE AUTHOR

TESSA DARE is the *New York Times* and *USA Today* bestselling author of thirteen historical romance novels and five novellas. Her books have won numerous accolades, including Romance Writers of America's prestigious RITA® Award and multiple *RT BOOKreviews* Reviewer's Choice Awards. *Booklist* magazine named her one of the "new stars of historical romance," and her books have been contracted for translation in twenty languages.

A librarian by training and a book-lover at heart, Tessa makes her home in Southern California, where she lives with her husband, their two children, and two cosmic kitties.

Discover great authors, exclusive offers, and more at hc.com.